"I'm ready."

Demi went in the therapy room, almost used to the sight of Colin's incredible physique all laid out for her to touch. *Almost.*

Candles lit, music on, hands oiled, she started with the sweeping motions that would improve circulation to his muscles. He was so much looser than when they started three weeks before. Unfortunately it was even more of a pleasure to touch him, and stupidly she gave in, allowing herself sensual enjoyment.

For some reason, as she worked, instead of loosening, his body stayed tight; his breathing picked up.

"You're not relaxing."

"I'm...a little uncomfortable." His voice was low.

"How can I help?"

"I could tell you exactly how." His tone was humorous. "But I'm pretty sure you wouldn't like the idea."

Demi's hands stilled. *Oh.* He was aroused. Because *she* was touching him? No, no, he could be enjoying her massage and fantasizing about anyone. Except, this was the first time she'd been so flustered.

And so tempted....

Blaze

Dear Reader,

It's always bittersweet when a miniseries ends. I get so fond of the characters, and even though I take care to send each couple off into the world's most romantic sunset, I do miss them. The Friends with Benefits quintet were particular favorites.

Feels So Right is physical therapist Demi Anderson's story. She was a bit of a mystery in the first two books (*Just One Kiss* and *Light Me Up*) and it was great fun for me to explore her more deeply. Having been a painfully shy kid myself, I know how hard it is to navigate certain social situations, even as an outwardly confident adult.

In injured Ironman triathlete Colin Russo, Demi finds a personal and professional challenge—like how to keep her hands off him when it's her job to touch him everywhere!—but he also helps her feel comfortable in her own skin. True love should always bring out one's better self.

I hope you have enjoyed this miniseries!

Cheers,

Isabel Sharpe

www.IsabelSharpe.com

Isabel Sharpe

FEELS SO RIGHT

HARLEQUIN®
entertain, enrich, inspire™

Recycling programs
for this product may
not exist in your area.

ISBN-13: 978-0-373-79718-9

FEELS SO RIGHT

www.Harlequin.com

Printed in U.S.A.

ABOUT THE AUTHOR

Isabel Sharpe was not born pen in hand like so many of her fellow writers. After she quit work to stay home with her firstborn son and nearly went out of her mind, she started writing. After more than twenty novels for Harlequin Books—along with another son—Isabel is more than happy with her choice these days. She loves hearing from readers. Write to her at www.isabelsharpe.com.

Books by Isabel Sharpe

HARLEQUIN BLAZE

186—THRILL ME†
221—ALL I WANT…**
244—WHAT HAVE I DONE FOR ME LATELY?
292—SECRET SANTA
     "The Nights Before Christmas"
376—MY WILDEST RIDE††
393—INDULGE ME§
444—NO HOLDING BACK
553—WHILE SHE WAS SLEEPING…§§
539—SURPRISE ME…§§
595—TURN UP THE HEAT~
606—LONG SLOW BURN~
619—HOT TO THE TOUCH~
678—JUST ONE KISS*
704—LIGHT ME UP*

†Do Not Disturb
**The Wrong Bed
††The Martini Dares
§Forbidden Fantasies
§§The Wrong Bed: Again & Again
~Checking E-Males
*Friends With Benefits

To get the inside scoop on Harlequin Blaze and its talented writers, be sure to check out blazeauthors.com.

To Dad, who would have read this one, too

1

ARGH, THE PHONE. Wasn't that always the way? After a long day at her physical-therapy practice, followed by a good hard run and a quick dinner, Demi was just settling in for a short relax-break with her knitting and an audiobook of a suspense novel. Her business line had been quiet for hours, but of course the second her butt hit her overstuffed, supercomfortable chair...

Local caller. She didn't recognize the number. "Demi Anderson."

"Yeah, hi." A deep male voice, familiar, but she couldn't place it. "This is Colin Russo. You treated me back in August."

Demi sat up straight, heart accelerating. Well, well. The cranky triathlete was back. After a few sessions for ruptured disc pain, and her confirmation of his doctor's bad news that he wouldn't be competing in any more Ironman triathlons, Colin had exploded with anger and frustration, and stalked out of her studio in search of a practitioner who'd tell him what he wanted to hear.

Yeah, good luck with that.

"Hi, Colin. What can I do for you?"

"I'd like to see you."

"Sure. Let me look at my schedule." She pulled up her calendar, wondering what had made him come back. Elite athletes took the longest to accept new limitations. If Colin had changed his attitude she could do him some good. Otherwise…

"On Thursday I have—"

"Anything sooner?" He was speaking in a clipped manner that suggested he was either angry or hurting. Probably both.

"You're in pain." She made sure she spoke matter-of-factly. Sympathy didn't go over well with these types.

"Yup." The syllable was abrupt.

"How about…" She ran over the next day's schedule. Busy, but she could give up her lunch hour. "Noon tomorrow?"

"Good."

"Okay, see you then." She hung up the phone and sat for a few quiet seconds, annoyed at the way her pulse was still racing, then jumped up and crossed to her window. She looked out at the street below, Olive Way where it intersected with Broadway in Seattle's Capitol Hill neighborhood. A few cars, headlights on. Not much traffic for a Monday evening. Maple leaves turning color, a light rain typical for October.

Colin Russo.

He'd been a challenge on multiple levels. Demi worked with and treated many athletes, had seen plenty of people hurting, plenty upset at having to confront lifestyle changes after an injury. Like other professionals in the medical field, she had to balance appropriate levels of caring and involvement with enough distance to keep clients' problems from taking her over. Colin had so bravely tried not to show his physical or emotional pain that his rage had touched her, though she'd been taken aback by the suddenness and intensity of the blowout. Humans who felt helpless often turned fear into anger.

Then there was that other problem, one Demi didn't like admitting. She'd found herself reacting physically to touching Colin's body, was too aware of his smooth skin, his remarkable athletic build, his masculine aftershave-and-soap smell. Found herself reacting emotionally to the way he betrayed discomfort only by tightness around his mouth or the occasional quicker-than-most breath. To the sleep-deprivation circles under his eyes, the low, sad set of his brows.

Demi prided herself on treating not only the injured part, but the whole person. Part of her job with Colin, as it had been with so many others, was to make him understand that injury didn't mean the end of his life. Eventually he would be able to compete in triathlons again—though substantially shorter ones. He'd be able to work, marry, have kids—all things vital to being human. This was a message she'd had to deliver many times to many people. She'd just never before pictured herself doing it with her body curled around the client to comfort him.

Part of her had been relieved when Colin disappeared. With any luck when she saw him this time, the unwelcome feelings would have disappeared, too. Luckily painful childhood shyness had made hiding herself second nature. Colin would never know she considered him hot enough to boil water.

A glance at her watch told her a meeting of the five Come to Your Senses building residents started soon. She just had time to call her friend and former client, Wesley, for his inevitable told-you-so. After Colin's dramatic exit in early September, Wesley had predicted with absolute certainty that he'd be back. Demi had been equally sure pride wouldn't let him return. The stakes had been the usual: coffee or a beer at their favorite café, Joe Bar on Roy Street.

She dialed, grinning. "Hey, Wesley. Good news for you. Colin Russo just called. Wants to come in tomorrow. You win."

"Ha!" Wesley's voice was jubilant. Demi had won the last two bets: whether a mom at Angela's bakery downstairs, where they were having coffee, would give in to her screaming toddler and buy him a cupcake—she didn't—and whether Wesley's ex-girlfriend would wear black to a mutual friend's wedding—she had. "I knew I'd win this one. He wasn't going to find hands like yours anywhere else."

"I don't know about that." She felt herself blushing and was very glad Wesley wasn't in the room. Something about Colin...

"Did he say why he was coming back?"

"Just that he was in pain and needed to see me. Must have been bad. He sounded as if he were talking through his teeth."

"Furious he had to crawl back to you."

"Could be." She immediately had to banish an image of Colin, shirtless, on his knees... "I can't talk long, got a Come to Your Senses meeting in a few. Just wanted to let you gloat."

"I'm gloating, I'm gloating. When do I get my drink at Joe Bar?"

"Whenever you want it." Like all introverts, she was protective of her alone time, but she always made the effort to see Wesley, a former marathoner. His running career had ended with a car accident—much worse than Colin's fall from his bike—and head injury that ensured he'd never run again, though he credited Demi with helping him relearn how to walk. For a brief time, maybe two weeks after his therapy ended, they'd tried dating, but it had never felt right and they'd happily gone back to being friends.

"What's tomorrow, Tuesday?" he asked. "I have a date. How about Wednesday?"

"Wednesday's fine. You seeing Cathy again?"

"Yup. See if she can fall in love with a guy who shuffles instead of walks."

Demi grimaced in sympathy. Wesley had been remarkably free of self-pity during his recovery, but it must be agony as a former athlete to walk as if he'd just learned how. Which he had in a way. "If she can't handle a good shuffle, she doesn't deserve you."

"You're a good person, Demi. Remind me why we're not dating?"

"I think it was the lack of desperate need to jump each other."

"Oh, right. That. We're not quite old enough to settle for peaceful companionship, huh."

Demi snorted. "I'm *never* going to be that old."

Wesley burst out laughing. "That's my sex fiend. Okay, go meet with your business partners. And don't let that Bonnie woman get to you."

"I promise." Demi grinned. Wesley was always watching out for her. Whoever he landed would be one lucky woman. She hoped Cathy had brains enough to see that. "Bonnie isn't terrible, she just doesn't know what to make of me. The woman is totally out there, and I'm totally in here."

"No excuse. She gives you any more trouble, let me know."

"See you Wednesday." She disconnected the call, put aside her knitting—a short-sleeved cotton sweater in an easy zigzag pattern for spring—and went in search of her shoes, which she found in her room, one on the floor, one on the bed where she'd kicked them off.

Ready. Sighing, she exited her second-floor apartment and headed down the hall. Bonnie had painted the walls with twining rose vines and, for Jack and Seth, who'd been disgusted by the girlie touch, a line of tanks along the baseboard. At the end of the hall was the apartment the five of them shared as a common area, though Demi didn't spend much time there.

Jack, Seth, Angela and Bonnie had been four of the original five University of Washington alumni who bought and renovated the building, naming it Come to Your Senses when they realized their five businesses represented the five senses. On the first floor was Angela's bakery, A Taste for All Pleasures. Across from that, Bonnie's flower shop, Bonnie Blooms, smelling wonderful. Farther down the hall, Jack Shea represented sight with his photography studio, and Demi's physical-therapy practice was all about touch. She'd bought the space from Caroline, one of the original five investors, who'd moved out of town to get married. Upstairs, Seth Blackstone—representing sound—lived and composed music in the largest of the apartments.

The other four residents were already seated in the spacious living room, drinking soda and/or beer from the refrigerator they all chipped in to keep stocked. Likewise they'd each donated old or unwanted chairs and tables to furnish the place. Feeling out of place and nervous as she always did around her building-mates, Demi grabbed a Sprite from the refrigerator and plunked down on the room's newest and ugliest piece, a black-and-white, futuristic leather love seat she'd gotten from one of her sister Carrie's I'm-bored-with-my-furniture remodeling fits.

Seth, Jack, Angela and Bonnie had been close friends for six years; they shared a boatload of history, in-jokes, stories—it was hard not to feel like an intruder. Given that Demi's shyness made her feel like an intruder in pretty much every social situation anyway, this one was particularly difficult. Angela had been sweet to her, as had Jack and occasionally Seth. Bonnie would be the toughest to melt, but Demi hadn't given up yet.

"Hey, Demi, how's it going?"

"Fine." She nodded stiffly at Angela; the chestnut-haired beauty was sitting on the beaten-up rocker in the corner of the room. The question always made Demi feel she should come up with thrilling new daily developments. The truth was, her life was pretty simple and pretty fulfilling—except in the romance department. It just didn't make good press.

Jack grinned at her from his signature overstuffed wreck of a chair. He'd always been friendly, but was much more relaxed and outgoing since he met and fell in love with a woman named Melissa. He'd been photographing her without her knowledge at Cal Anderson Park for weeks before she walked into his shop, saw pictures of herself and freaked out. Happily, he'd quickly gained her trust and eventually her heart. "How's things in the physical-therapy world?"

"Okay. Thanks." She felt herself blushing, hating the stilted way she spoke, hating the awkwardness that had risen inside her since she was a child, which made the easy banter others took for granted so impossible for her. Once she was comfortable with people, once she trusted them, she was fine. But with Bonnie all but rolling her eyes at Demi's presence in the room, she couldn't unbend enough to sound like a normal person. Which of course made Bonnie's scorn worse. "People keep getting hurt. Keep needing me."

"Have you seen that gorgeous guy again?" Angela was all ears. "If he's been around lately I've missed him."

"Colin?" Demi felt a funny jolt of adrenaline. How weird

that Angela would bring him up today. "I'm seeing him at noon tomorrow."

"Ooh!" Angela waggled her eyebrows. "Bonnie, we're going to have to line up in the hallway and watch this one go by."

"I have to take a rain check." Bonnie shook her head regretfully, glancing at Seth, who sat next to her on the old green couch. "I have a lunch date tomorrow."

"Yeah? What's this one? Garbage man? Prison guard?" Seth tried to look casually interested, but was clearly wary, or at least it seemed that way to Demi. Seth and Bonnie— some romantic history there, Demi was sure of it. Sparks and intimacy flew between them, and whenever they were together they were either fighting or laughing, never indifferent. But with Bonnie signed up on Seattledates.com, they must be on the outs.

"His name is Don." Bonnie lifted her chin, smoothing folds of her bright, outrageously patterned top. "He's a lawyer."

"A *lawyer.*" Jack rolled his eyes. "*That'll* be fascinating conversation."

"Maybe he'll show you his briefs," Seth added.

"Oh, that is just the *most* clever line I've ever heard a *million* times." Bonnie sighed.

"Yeah, it was lame." Seth hoisted himself off the couch, stretching his over-six-foot lean frame. "I must need another beer. You want anything, Bon?"

"No. Thanks, Seth." Bonnie glanced tenderly at his back; she was clearly capable of deep loyalty and affection—just not for Demi.

"Good luck, Bonnie," Jack said. "You certainly deserve a normal experience."

"No kidding." She rolled her green eyes. "It's been one disaster after another."

A snort from Seth, who was at the refrigerator. "Anyone else need anything?"

"No, thanks." Angela opened a folder on her lap. "But I have an idea I want to share with you guys. Actually Melissa got me thinking about it."

"Uh-oh." Jack's dark eyes turned warm. He was totally hot anyway, and looked even hotter when he thought about Melissa. Demi wouldn't mind some guy turning liquid on her behalf. She'd had one long-term boyfriend in college, one a few years after, then some casual dating but nothing for a while. At twenty-eight, she was starting to wonder about settling down, having babies, the whole deal. Too bad she couldn't just snap her fingers and find the perfect mate. That's what her older brother and sister had done, once again demonstrating their ability to sail effortlessly through life. She had no idea how they did it. Everything she accomplished seemed to require superhuman effort.

"Last summer Melissa had that idea about making Come to Your Senses a one-stop bridal-pampering place, remember?"

"I loved the idea." Bonnie nodded enthusiastically. "Flowers from me, cake or pastry from Angela, a portrait by Jack and music from Seth, our very own YouTube sensation."

And…? Demi sat silent, not able to tell if the omission was deliberate, unsure whether pointing it out would make things better or worse.

"And a massage from Demi," Angela prompted gently.

"Right." Bonnie thwacked her forehead. "Sorry, Demi. I forgot you."

"'S'okay." Demi kept her eyes down. The closest she and Bonnie had gotten to friendliness was when Angela and Bonnie bumped into her on their way to go dancing one evening last summer and had dragged her along. It had been one of the most fun nights Demi'd had in a while. She loved to dance. That night alcohol and circumstances had made Bonnie actually pleasant, a start Demi had hoped they could build on afterward.

Not so much.

"So, anyway." Angela broke the awkward silence. "I was thinking we could take the same package idea, but have it available as a holiday special from Thanksgiving through New Year's Day. We can charge a flat rate and sell certificates people can buy for themselves or as a gift. What do you think?"

"Wow. I love that idea!" Bonnie grinned, eyes alight, and looked at Seth and Jack for their reactions.

"Same here," Jack said. "Get us new business and reward our existing customers. Win-win."

"I was talking with Daniel about it last night as a wedding package and whining that we'd missed the summer bridal rush and then it came to me...the holidays!"

"I love the idea, Angela." Demi smiled at her. She looked so amazingly happy these days. Last spring she'd fallen for a guy who'd come into her bakery for white cupcakes to commemorate his late fiancée's birthday. Angela had sneaked in a chocolate cupcake to cheer Daniel up, and ended up doing a lot more than that. On her right hand she wore his diamond promise ring. "It's brilliant."

"I've got the perfect jingle." Seth got a faraway look in his narrow gray eyes, then cleared his throat and started a jazzy tune. *"Spend holiday money on your sweetest honey. The cash you've paid will ensure you get lai—"*

"Stop!" Angela and Bonnie yelled at the same time, then tried to restrain their giggles.

"What? What did I do?" Seth dropped his innocent look for a grin and squeezed Bonnie's shoulder. "Okay, maybe it needs work."

"We should plan this out." Angela started counting on her fingers. "Make posters, work on a jingle for a radio spot—G-rated, thank you, Seth. I also think it's time to bite the bullet and come up with a communal website. Right now we each have our own. What do you think?"

There was general assent, lots of joking, lots of constructive brainstorming and thorough planning. Demi was, as always, impressed by the quartet she'd signed on with. They worked hard and had all done well, though she wasn't sure about Bonnie, who always went oddly quiet when the others discussed their good fortune. She'd also dropped quite a bit of weight in the last six months or so and never seemed terribly busy in her shop. Demi hoped she was just angsting about her romantic life. Maybe she'd fall in love with a nice rich guy. Demi's sister had done that. Boy had she. And didn't let anyone forget it for more than twenty seconds.

The meeting broke up; Demi left the four of them still chatting. She was tired, anxious to get to bed, a little flustered at the idea of seeing Colin again the next day. Often she'd dream about whatever she concentrated on at night, powerful dreams that affected her the whole next day. Tonight before she went to bed, she'd imagine him toothless with bugs crawling all over him. That way she might be able to turn him into an object of disgust.

Yeah, and if *that* worked, she'd try walking on water next.

Half an hour later, she was snuggled in bed, listening to the October rain tap on the window, concentrating on Colin, not the way he was, but the way she wanted to dream about him.

Big brown eyes—make those piggy, puffy red ones. His fabulous male scent—now eau de skunky hangover. His rare smile—brown and broken. His build—flabtastic.

Plaid pants, platform shoes. Flowered shirt unbuttoned to his waist.

Gold chains…

She gave a huge yawn and nestled deeper under the covers, smiling faintly.

Long, greasy hair.

Another yawn. Take that, Colin…

Morning already? Couldn't be. Somehow Demi was in her office suite without getting out of bed. Her waiting room, normally a cool, refreshing blue-green color, had been repainted violet with rainbows and pictures of clowns. She glanced at her watch, not the gold one she'd bought for herself, but pink glowing plastic with a picture of Barbie on it. Noon! Colin was about to show up.

A knock on the door. She tried to say, "Come in," but couldn't make a sound. The door opened. Colin! Except he was about four foot five, wearing a clown costume—white with huge red dots and yellow ruffles, floppy black shoes, giant red nose.

This must be her dream. Perfect.

Lie down, she told him without sound. *I'll work on you.*

"Sure." His voice emerged without problem, deep, resonant, very sexy. Oops, she'd forgotten to change that to an appropriately girlie squeak.

You can keep your clown suit on.

"No." He moved his hands to the back of his suit.

She tried to say yes, but couldn't make herself understood, and frowned at him instead, frantically gesturing that he should stop.

Wait, was he growing taller? He was, no! Taller than she was, up to his real height, just over six feet.

Bad clown, bad.

The silly suit melted off. Instead of proper clown underwear, he was wearing boxer briefs that molded to a decidedly not flabby body. The violet walls changed to trees, and suddenly Demi and Colin were lying in a meadow on a blanket, picnic basket nearby, holding glasses of champagne.

Uh-oh.

Then the champagne was gone and he was kissing her tenderly, his body warm and solid against the length of hers…which no longer had any clothes on it. And his briefs were gone, too.

Oh, no.

His mouth tasted hers languidly—upper lip, bottom lip, this corner, that. Then he pulled back and gazed at her from under his brows, causing her blood to race, her body to arch toward his.

Oh, yes.

He rolled over her, the width of his shoulders making her feel protected, surrounded. She felt him hard between her legs, opened hers wide to welcome him inside.

Then he was pushing into her, filling, stretching, setting her nerve endings on fire. She clasped him around the back, lifted her knees high and wide to bring him in deeper.

He said her name over and over, increasing the pressure and pace until she was gasping, reaching for her climax, reaching, reaching, feeling it start to grow, to burn through—

"Demi, I love you."

Say what?

Demi woke with a jerk, staring with wide eyes up at the ceiling, breath coming fast, body still hot with arousal. Instinctively, her hand went between her legs, and then she stopped herself.

No.

There was no way she could get herself off right now. Because if she did, she'd be imagining Colin making her completely crazy with lust, and when he showed up for real in—she blinked at the clock—six hours, there would be no way she could look him in the eye. And no way she could put her hands on his back and think of anything but the way she'd clasped that same back while he was hot and hard inside her.

Bad, bad clown.

COLIN WOKE WITH a jerk, staring with wide eyes up at his ceiling, breath coming fast.

A dream. Damn it all to hell. He'd been on the last leg of the Ironman World Championship triathlon in Hawaii. He'd already sailed through the two-point-four-mile swim, powered through the one-hundred-twelve-mile bike ride and was approaching the finish line after the twenty-six-mile marathon barely out of breath, legs still strong, in first place by a hundred feet.

What a high. What a feeling. His body ultrafit, lean and strong. All those hours, all those years of training, coming down to this one explosive sprint to victory that would make him world champion. Just him, on top of the field, the dense crowd at the finish line already cheering for him. Stephanie was there, too, long blond hair swept back in a ponytail, blue eyes glowing, beaming with pride. Her man was number one and she was crazy about him.

Then he'd woken up, not on a triumphant path to victory, but in bed, back muscles contorting in agony, pain shooting down his right leg.

From king of fitness to short-term disability after falling off his bike like a six-year-old just learning to ride.

They said he was done. They said his back was too messed up ever to be able to ride long hours bent over his handlebars. They said disc injuries like his could be controlled but not healed.

Bull. Maybe some people could hear "no" and accept it, but Colin wasn't one of them. "No" just meant he'd have to work harder, train harder. Fine by him. He was no stranger to hard work.

But he shouldn't have tried to get back to training so soon. Demi had been right, damn it. He'd left her in exasperation last summer, disgusted that an athlete of his caliber should be doing exercises a couch potato could do without effort. Infuriated by her insistence he'd have to cut his recovery expectations to a more "realistic" level. Frustrated that she didn't understand why his level of fitness couldn't be compromised, not now, not this year, not when he had so much to accomplish. So he'd left. Tried another therapist, then another, both of whom had babied him even worse than Demi had. Finally he'd decided he could manage his own damn recovery. Who knew his body better than he did?

Pain shot through him, and he tried like hell to breathe through it, not to tense into the spasms, which made them worse.

Yeah, guess what, managing his own recovery had been a bad idea. Everything sounded like a bad idea these days. Including going back to see Demi.

Because there was another reason he'd left her. By the last of—what was it, three, four appointments? maybe five?—he'd spent the entire session desperately trying to keep from having an erection. He had no idea what she did to him, but it was hell. Demi couldn't hold a candle to his ex-girlfriend Stephanie's fresh California-girl beauty. Demi was dark; he preferred blondes. And she was withdrawn, where he liked a woman with spirit. She was decently attractive, but not beautiful, with wide eyes and a faint cleft in her chin. She had style and grace to burn, and she exuded peace that both stirred and soothed him.

And her hands…

Not going to think about that. The only thing on his mind in her studio today would be multiplication tables and baseball statistics. Unless the crazy attraction had run its course and he'd react more normally this time. That would be good.

He waited for the attack of pain to subside, then drew one knee up slowly toward his chest to stretch, barely able to get it halfway. His flexibility was crap. He couldn't work. Couldn't train.

This sucked.

Yeah, he was being a big poor-me baby, so sue him. He had good reason.

His cell rang. The act of twisting his head to locate his phone on the bedside table caused another spasm, this time in his neck and upper back.

Thirty-four years old and he was falling apart.

Gritting his teeth against the pain, he picked up the phone. Nick. His erstwhile training partner, and the other half of the collision that had pitched Colin off his bike. Nick had skinned his knees. Not that Colin would ever wish this injury on anyone else, but sometimes life was damn unfair.

He took a deep breath, willing his voice to sound normal. "Hey, man."

"How's it going?"

"Not bad." He didn't dare use long sentences in case he had to break off and groan in agony.

"John and I are going to run some hills. Wondered if you'd like to meet up for lunch after."

Yeah, he'd love to. Sit there, the sad cripple, while they exulted in how well their training was going.

"Can't today. Got an appointment."

"Yeah? You back at work?"

"Nah. Physical therapy."

"Dude, you're doing that again?"

"Yup." He didn't feel like explaining.

"Okay. So, uh…" He cleared his throat awkwardly. "You heard from Stephanie lately?"

"Nope." This conversation was not making him feel any better. His girlfriend of four years had gotten sick of his bad attitude and his misery and dumped him on his ass, ironically just as he was seriously considering giving her what she wanted: a proposal.

Stephanie was a marathoner and they'd done a lot of training together. Colin should have noticed how hard it was on her that he was suffering, but he'd been a selfish jerk for quite a few months now. He figured it was only a matter of time before Stephanie came back to him. No doubt in his mind that he could make things right when she cooled off. She loved him. He loved her. They liked the same things, shared friends—at least they had before the breakup. What more did they need? Maybe the relationship had gotten a little stale, but the initial excitement never lasted. He needed to settle down if he wanted kids, which he did, and Stephanie would make a good mom and a solid partner.

One thing at a time. "Have a good lunch, Nick. Maybe I'll be up for it next time."

"Sure. Sure." His tone made it clear he wasn't holding his breath. "Nice talking to you."

"Same." No, it hadn't been nice for Nick. It wasn't nice for anyone to talk to Colin lately. His mom had told him he needed to see a shrink. Dad, predictably, told him to suck it up and be a man.

Yeah, well, he'd never been the kind of man Dad wanted him to be, so why start now?

He closed his eyes, smiling grimly. His level of cranky misery was even disgusting him.

After a few more careful stretches he'd loosened his

muscles to the point where he could just manage to get out of bed. A stunning victory, one that lifted his spirits at least a little. The visit to Demi, if she could help him, would do more of the same.

For the past decade Colin's pursuit of physical power and endurance had dominated his life. He'd been something of a missionary about the miracle of fitness, becoming a personal trainer to help others find the same high of good health and solid self-esteem he'd been able to achieve through working his body.

Now what he could reclaim of his old life rested in the talented hands of a woman he'd sworn never to cross paths with again.

2

DEMI GLANCED AT the clock on the wall of her office, embarrassed to be so jittery. Two more minutes until Colin arrived. *Stay cool, girlfriend.* He was just another client, a man in pain, one of the many she'd treated, one she'd be able to help. For today she'd ignore her whole-client philosophy and concentrate on seeing his body as a collection of muscles, tendons and bones. There would be time for worrying about his brain later—if he stuck with the therapy.

Mysterious, this upset to her system. Demi knew what kind of guy attracted her, and the überjock was definitely not it. Besides, Colin had a serious girlfriend. Sharon or Tiffany or something. A marathoner. Not that he'd look at a woman like Demi twice anyway, especially after she'd pissed him off so badly last time by gently trying to get him to face the truth about his recovery—or lack thereof.

Another glance at the clock. One more minute. Would he be out in her waiting area already? Her studio space, originally a two-bedroom apartment, had been renovated into a waiting room, office, one small room for examination and massage and a larger one for exercising, with a gym mat, treadmill, stationary bike, and the free weights, balls and other tools of her trade.

The minute hand of the clock joined the hour hand at twelve. She gave up her rather lame attempt at updating her previous client's file and stood. *Ready, set, go.* Reminding herself of Colin's anger and poorly hidden contempt at their last meeting, she lifted her chin and opened the door to the waiting room.

Her body went on an immediate adrenaline fizz.

Yeah, he was there. And he was still gorgeous.

At least she'd prepared herself. The first time she'd opened this same door to him back in August, she'd been so flustered by the intensity of his brown eyes and the sheer beautiful size and shape of him, she'd blushed, dropped her gaze and mumbled like a complete geekazoid.

"Colin, hi, come on in." She smiled and gestured toward her massage room, this time blushless, in control and professional.

He nodded and stood slowly, hitches in the motion indicating muscles lashing out at him.

"Uh-oh." Demi's smile faded when she saw what the movement cost him. "You don't look so good. Bad pain?"

"It's—" His response was cut short by what must have been a killer spasm. "Not the greatest."

Translation for a normal human: nearly unbearable. When it came to pain, elite athletes spoke a different language.

"I'll work on that today—should be able to give you some relief." She followed him into the small room where she did her massages. Decorwise, she'd worked to achieve a balance between clinical and luxurious. Half examining room, half spa, with softer lighting than one would expect from a medical office, and nice touches like fresh flowers courtesy of Bonnie Blooms, a CD player for music and a light scent she sprayed on the bedding, floral for women, spice for men. "You know the routine. As many clothes off as you're comfortable with, under the sheet on your stomach. If you need help getting on the table, yell and I'll come in."

"Right."

She smiled and left the room, waiting outside the door, knowing he wouldn't call even if he was in agony. Honestly. What an ego. Risking serious injury to avoid asking for help? Crazy. But he wasn't the first and wouldn't be the last. She'd gotten used to people's peculiarities. Women who hated being touched, men who liked it way too much...

"Ready," he called. Sooner than she'd expected.

She waited three beats and went in. Colin lay with the sheet down to his waist, shoulders as broad as the table, looking like a sexual invitation—or he would if his body wasn't stiff with pain. She eased a cushion under his hips to relieve pressure on his back, opened her heated cabinet and took out a blanket, pulled the sheet up to his neck and draped the warm cover over him. She was glad to hide him from view while she collected herself, cranky that this difficult man provoked such a strong reaction and that she couldn't seem to control it.

Heading for the hand sanitizer she abruptly rechanneled her brain when she found herself wondering how much Colin was still wearing under the sheet. "How have you been?"

"Fabulous," he growled.

Ah. Still Mr. Sunshine. Okay, then. She'd stick with his physical problems today, give him some relief and worry about the rest of him another time if he gave her that chance. "Can you describe your pain? Any particular location?"

"Down my right leg. Neck. Shoulders. Back."

"Doesn't leave much, does it." She suppressed a very tempting told-you-so and turned on her CD player, which filled the room with a bland but relaxing tune she'd heard so many times it barely registered. "The leg pain is from nerves pinched by the disc bulging in your spine. The rest is sympathetic reaction from other muscles, which—"

"I know where the pain comes from."

Grrr. Demi sent him a poisoned glance he couldn't see. Lovely, lovely man. Just as well. If he had an appealing personality to go with those looks and that body, he'd be much too dangerous to have around. Not fair for one person to have that much going for him, anyway. "I'll see what I can do today about loosening you up."

"That would be good." His voice was softer.

Well. Not exactly charming, but better. Demi pulled her bottle of peppermint-scented oil from its warming stand and poured some onto her hands, concentrating on the familiar routine. "I'll start with a light massage, then we'll go deeper. You let me know when it's too much."

As if he would. She could probably light matches and stick them under his fingernails and he'd pretend not to notice.

"Okay." His voice was strained now.

Hands oiled, she had no further excuse to avoid touching him.

So.

This was about his back. Just a back. She'd seen many beautiful backs before, athletic and otherwise. This was nothing different.

Demi laid her hands on him gently, started light sweeping motions following the muscles, encouraging blood flow and warmth, forcing her mind to register only the muscular system beneath her fingers. Trapezius. Latissimus dorsi. Deltoid. Teres major and minor.

So far so good, but she was keeping her movements brisk and mechanical, something she generally avoided. Slow stroking did a lot to bring comfort and pleasure to people in pain. Colin was a client like any other, and Demi wanted to bring him that pleasure.

Uh. She should not have phrased it that way.

Lips determinedly tight, she slowed her movements, traced his muscles more sensually. Colin needed as much TLC as anyone, maybe more, since the macho guys seldom knew they needed it and even fewer knew how to ask for it.

Her fingers relaxed into the slow pace of the music. She dipped them again in the peppermint-scented oil and moved up into his neck, appalled at the tension. This guy was suffering.

Back and neck warmed up, she moved downward to his gluteal muscles, blocking out the fact that he wasn't wearing anything but skin under the sheet, blocking out any picture in her brain but those suitable for an anatomy class, because otherwise her thoughts would go down an entirely different path.

They did anyway. Colin let out a groan of pleasure, and Demi had the absurd urge to lean down and press her lips to the small of his back, let her hair sweep over his—

For heaven's sake.

Gluteus maximus. Largest of the butt muscles, supporting the pelvis, vital in maintaining an erect—

Torso, Demi. Torso.

Moving on, probably sooner than she should have, she swept over the long muscles in the backs of his thighs, the biceps femoris. He seemed to be lying easier now, already more relaxed.

"Better?" She moved up toward his back again. "I'm going to go deeper now, put strong pressure on the spasming muscles. It won't feel good while I'm doing it, but you'll heal faster in the long run."

"I can take it."

Demi rolled her eyes. Of course he could. She could drop

an anvil on his head and he'd insist it was a mild bruise. Guys like him reminded her of the scene in *Monty Python and the Holy Grail,* one of Wesley's favorite movies, in which a battling knight with amputated limbs insisted he was suffering only a flesh wound.

The next part would be a lot easier on her nerves. Neuromuscular therapy was substantially less sensual than the stroking involved in Swedish, and she had hard work to do, going for the most problematic muscles with fingers, fist or elbow, holding strong pressure until they relaxed and gave. Slowly, carefully, she worked on him, finding the process deeply satisfying. Time flew, and she managed to keep her thoughts strictly G-rated.

Well…maybe PG. One PG-13 when she was working on his butt the second time.

"Okay." She trailed light fingers over his back, then laid a firm hand between his shoulder blades before she lifted it off. Done. It was over. She'd survived. "You'll be sore tomorrow, maybe the next day, but after that you should start feeling looser."

He lifted his head, turned it experimentally, pushed cautiously up onto his elbows. She covered his body immediately with the sheet and blanket. "Feels better already."

"Good." Ooh, he'd said nearly a whole sentence. "We'll do this again, then get you to where you can start on some exercises."

"Gee, really?" He rolled cautiously onto his side. "Ten whole minutes on a stationary bike? Two or three sets of leg lifts?"

Grrr. "Gotta start somewhere, Colin."

"I know, I know." He lowered his head back down to the table. "Sorry."

The word came out as if it hurt worse than his back, but it did come out, and made him human enough for Demi to experience a quick pang of empathy. "In the shape you're in, you'll come back fast, Colin. Sprint triathlons are a sure thing, I'm betting within the year."

He grunted and managed to sit up, keeping the sheet safely tucked around his lower half.

Unfortunately, this gave her a superb view of his impressive chest. She spun around and busied herself arranging the scent bottles on her counter, which were already neatly arranged. Sprint triathlons were a hell of a comedown for someone hoping to qualify for the Ironman World Championship. A quarter-mile swim, twelve-to-fifteen-mile bike ride and three-mile run. He could do that in his sleep.

"I know. Doesn't seem much of a challenge. But it's better than being out of the circuit entirely."

"Whatever."

Demi should have known better. Colin was still grieving hard over his loss; he wasn't ready to see any of the positives yet.

"You should be able to whip a couple of old ladies your first time out." She held up a hand. "I know, I know. You think I'm just trying to build your hopes up, but I'm not kidding."

Astoundingly, she heard the beginning of a chuckle. "Don't even talk to me."

Demi handed him a bottle of cold water, grinning. "Come into my office when you're dressed."

"Right."

She left the room and strode into her office, congratulating herself. *Excellent job, Demi Anderson.* A whole hour and she hadn't once sexually harassed him. A fine day's work. She should call Wesley or her friend Julie and go out for a celebratory drink. *Guess what? I had Colin Russo in my office and didn't grab his crotch! Yay!*

She giggled, imagining their faces, and wrote some notes

on Colin's chart, not that she was liable to forget their session by the next appointment—if he came back.

In pain. Uncommunicative. Hotter than a blast furnace. Identifies self strongly as triathlete. Must work on emotional acceptance of injury and its fallout as well as standard treatment for L4-L5 disc rupture.

Okay, she didn't really write the part about the blast furnace.

"I'm here."

She looked up, still refusing to blush, and gestured Colin into the chair set in front of her desk, wishing she'd thought to move it back several feet. But at least being behind the desk gave her a feeling of safety and authority. "You're moving easier."

"I feel better." He sat without as much effort as he'd used to stand, and rested his hands easily on his thighs. Demi felt as if the walls of her office had closed in a foot at least.

"You'll want to be on anti-inflammatories the next couple of days."

"Okay." He held her gaze steadily, as if he expected something from her. Demi opened his file, picked up a pen, took off the cap, wrote, *What the heck is he thinking?* in her most professional scrawl, then put the pen down.

"Colin, maybe we should talk about why you left. Why you came back. What you want from me and this treatment and how you feel about both."

"My feelings?" He looked disgusted. "This is *physical* therapy, right?"

Grrr. Demi needed to set boundaries right now or this would never end. Taking her sweet time responding, she leaned back in her chair and pretended to study his file. "You probably didn't know this, but I'm a betting woman."

"And…"

"And I bet I can tell you exactly how much your parents enjoyed your teenage years."

His silence made her wonder if she'd pushed too far, if they were about to embark on Colin Russo Tantrum, Part II. But when she glanced up again, he was looking amused for the first time. The expression changed his whole demeanor, got rid of the grouchy-brows and downturned mouth, relaxed his forehead and eyes. And made him even better looking, less sulky and more vibrantly male. She could only begin to imagine his magnetism when he was operating at one hundred percent. "I was hell on wheels."

"Not surprised."

"I still am, I know that. This is not easy."

"I am not suggesting it is, or that it should be."

"But I don't need to beat you up with it?"

She shrugged. "I think I could do you more good without that, yes."

"Okay."

Demi raised her eyebrows. "It's that easy? I say 'please play nice' and you do?"

"I tried doing this my way, and figured out when I could barely get out of bed this morning for the fifth time this month that my way doesn't work. My body isn't behaving the way it has for the past thirty-four years. The rules have changed. I have to get to know a new person but it's still me."

"It won't always be this bad. But yes, it's tough for athletes. You have such intimate knowledge of bodies—your bodies." Oh, geez. Did she have to phrase it that way? He looked mildly surprised, still amused, his deep brown eyes intently focused on her. Demi was so flustered she had to look back down at his file. "Now that has changed, you'll have to form a different kind of intimate…relationship."

Stop. Just stop right now. Except he wasn't saying anything and she couldn't stand silence.

"I know you can do it." She closed his file, folded her hands on top of it and determinedly met his eyes again—then wished she hadn't when she found them full of mischief. Her brain mushed on her. "Your discipline is already there. It's just a change. You won't be able to stay training... to keep so hard anymore. Hard on *yourself.*"

Okay, her face was officially on fire. All pretense at cool was gone.

"I give up." She lifted her hands, let them smack down on her desk. "You're hurting but it will get better. That's all I'm trying to say."

He was chuckling for real now, his face relaxing further. "I think it was funnier when you were telling me I'd have trouble staying hard again."

"No, no." She shook her head, hands up and out. "That is not my expertise. If you'd like me to help with your pain and the management of your injury, I can. But only if you are realistic about what we can accomplish and how far you can come back. That's going to be much more difficult than the rest of it."

His expression turned grim again. "So I'm discovering."

"Now." Demi composed herself, relieved they were back on familiar ground. "You're a personal trainer and health-club manager."

"Was." His jaw set again. "Will be again."

"You enjoy it?"

"When I can do it, yeah."

She nodded thoughtfully. "The first thing we need to focus on is getting you out of this rut of only thinking about things you can't do. To all my clients I preach the gospel trinity. Positive thinking, can-do attitudes and silver linings. These are the only ways your life can become better after a big change like this."

"Right."

She expected the cynical reaction. "Any hobbies?"

"Swimming, biking and running."

"Uh-huh." Somehow she kept from gritting her teeth. "Anything you did before you took up triathlons? Something you'd enjoy rediscovering?"

His eyes lit for a brief moment before he could resolutely shut down into misery again. Aha. There was something. Good thing, because he definitely needed a jump start back into feeling productive.

"I used to play alto sax." He laughed without humor and shrugged. "I was pretty bad."

"Doesn't matter. If you still have the instrument, bring it by in a week or so when you're standing easier. What else?"

His eyes narrowed. "Bring it here?"

She returned his gaze calmly. Was he going to fight her on everything? "How much does an alto sax weigh, about ten pounds?"

"Not quite."

"Heavy enough. I want to watch you play to make sure you're handling the instrument in a way that isn't going to sabotage your progress. What else?"

His expression grew darker; clearly he thought her questions a waste of time. She had to remind herself to focus on that glimmer of mischief and good humor that had transformed him. She wanted to bring that man back, healed, whole and happy. Because if he stayed like this, she was going to have to medicate herself to be anywhere near him.

"I used to have another hobby."

"Yes…?"

"I made knives."

"Knives." She wasn't sure what to think about that. "Tell me more."

"More?" He shrugged. "I made knives."

Grrr. Just talk to me. "What kind?"

"Kitchen, hunting, whatever."

"You make them from scratch? Blade and everything?"

"Everything." A glint of pride. "Handle, blade…yes."

"How cool." She let the silence go a few seconds. "Why did you stop?"

"Ran out of time."

"Would you say making knives brought you some of the same satisfaction as—"

"Here we go again." He sent her a mocking look. "Is this *physical* therapy or—"

"Okay, okay." She waved his question away. "My point is—"

"That my life isn't over. I have plenty to live for, and though it might seem bleak right now it's always darkest before the dawn and the world is my oyster."

"Colin." She looked at him disapprovingly. "You forgot every cloud has a silver lining and when God closes a door He opens a window."

He actually grinned at that, making him even more irresistible. "I guess I did."

"All joking aside, positive thinking, can-do attitudes and looking for silver linings are the tenets my practice is built on, so you can expect to hear about them until you're ready to scream. When do you want to come back?" She pulled her calendar up on her iPhone before he could make fun of her again. "Next week I've got Wednesday open at two o'clock."

"I'll take it."

"Good." She stood. "We'll make progress. Just please don't push between now and then. Once the pain is gone, and I mean gone, not bearable, you can ride your bike ten or fifteen minutes, easy, sitting up straight. If that goes well, we'll increase. Also, once the pain is gone, do a few, just a few, core exercises to keep those muscles from deteriorating too far. We need them strong to keep the pressure off your spine."

"Right."

"No cheating. No superhuman stuff. Baby steps at the beginning until the swelling is down."

"Right." He walked to the door, obviously in a hurry to escape her lecture, which, perversely, made her talk faster.

"Heat if you're stiff. Ice if the pain seems new."

"Right."

"Colin." Instead of kicking him in the gluteals, which she wanted to do, she gave him an encouraging smile, trying for supportive counselor and trusted medical adviser. "You're going to be okay. Better than okay. You're going to—"

"Right." He opened her door and took off down the hall, still walking stiffly but looser than when he came in.

Demi strode back into her office, closed the door and slumped against it. Colin was going to be tough. She wanted to heal him and let him see enough progress that he could shake off his despair. He needed self-motivation and spirit to do the hard work of fighting back to his new normal. She hoped she could be enough coach, inspiration and taskmaster to help him—while keeping herself and her goofy crush under control.

Every part of her hoped that Colin's recovery was smooth and quick. For his sake and hers.

Because if it wasn't, there was a good chance one of them would lose it.

3

"HEY, BONNIE, how's it going?"

Bonnie turned from a bucket of irises she was arranging in her shop, Bonnie Blooms, and grinned at Seth. He looked devastatingly handsome as usual in jeans and a gray shirt that matched his eyes. He could have been a model if he hadn't wanted to be a musician. "Hey, there."

Nothing in the world gave her as much pleasure as being able to greet Seth without feeling wistful and lovesick. Five years ago they'd broken up, after one year of dating in college that ended when Bonnie got serious and Seth got itchy. Since then, especially once they'd both moved into the Come to Your Senses building, they'd been dancing a painful and cautious circles-around-each-other minuet that had ended last August when Bonnie had finally, *finally* signed up for Seattledates.com.

Not only that, but now, a month and a half later, after many disasters, some comical, some cringe-worthy, most just bland, she'd finally, *finally* had a good date. A really good date. Extremely fun, in fact, with Don Stemper. She'd dated a few guys in the five years since she and Seth broke up, but this was the first time she had her head together and could give a new relationship one hundred percent.

"What's happening?"

She glanced pointedly at the flowers in her hands. "I'm arranging irises. What's happening with you?"

"I'm standing here talking to you."

"Ha-ha." She cut off an inch from one stem and replaced the bloom in water. Her shop was full of buckets of various flowers set at different levels, to give the shopper the impression that he or she had just walked into a carefully landscaped garden or an outdoor flower market. Bonnie was incredibly pleased with the effect. Unfortunately shoppers hadn't exactly been showing up in droves. Wedding season, in full tilt over the summer, had tided her over, brought some of her debt under control, and she was almost current on her payments, but business had slowed again, and she was in no shape to ride out bad times.

The one downside of her life right now, which she didn't like thinking about.

"You seen that guy again?" Seth spoke so ultracasually she knew immediately whom he meant.

"Don?"

"Yeah, whoever." He was practically growling, eyes stormy, his short, dark hair even more disheveled than usual, as if he'd been yanking on it all morning while composing his songs—a sure sign he was upset.

Bonnie wished she could feel vindictive and triumphant at the switch—for a change, *she* was moving on and *he* was left behind. Instead, she felt tender and guilty. Guilty? Ha! As if! She had nothing to feel guilty about. Seth had ended their relationship, not her. He was the one with the issues. If he was still in love with her and wanted her, he knew how to get her back. With a big fat until-death-do-us-part commitment. Bonnie would trust nothing less. But he'd shown no signs of wanting anything more than to get all stressed out about her decision to date, though to his credit, he'd done nothing to dissuade her and seemed to understand and support her decision.

They'd had one good nostalgic tumble in August, a strangely freeing experience that had been, in effect, a goodbye.

Mmm. A damn good nostalgic tumble. She'd been bent over the arm of the couch with her legs hooked around his back and he'd been—

Oof. Better not to think about that.

"Remember Matti?"

"Matti?" Of course she did. One of those unbearably gorgeous "friends" Seth kept coming up with. This one he'd bumped into in a bar, which apparently in his world constituted friendship. Matti had been interested in renting space in Bonnie's shop to sell perfume, which would have been incredibly helpful to Bonnie's bottom line. She'd agreed to consider it after Seth assured her he wasn't out for Matti's "bottom line" himself. "Nope, never heard of her."

"The perfume lady."

"Ohhh." Bonnie repositioned a group of alstroemeria in its bucket, pretending to be only half listening. For too long she'd hung on to Seth's every word, eagerly looking for any possible sign that he was weakening, that he realized how special their relationship was, that he wanted to take it to the next level. In the past six months, he'd seemed to be making snail's-pace progress, but she had been hurt too many times to trust any of it. "Yes, I remember now. What's happening with her?"

"She decided not to rent space in your shop. Sorry about that."

Bonnie rolled her eyes. "Given that it's been over a month since you mentioned her, I'm not exactly shocked."

"Not a month." He looked stunned. "Has it been? I thought it was— Wait…"

She laughed, shaking her head. "Someone's had his brain immersed in his music."

"I guess." He pulled a pink rose out of a nearby bucket and handed it to her. "For you."

"Awww, thanks, Seth." She made a big show of rolling her eyes, cursing her traitor heart for beating the tiniest bit faster when he handed her the flower.

"I was thinking…"

She snorted. "Don't strain anything."

"I have the perfect Christmas present for you."

Bonnie stiffened. Oh, no. He was not going to start with this seduction crap again, was he? Not that it mattered. She had Don to think about now, to fantasize about, to talk to and confide in. His profile had said he was looking for marriage, right there in black and white, and wow, men could do that? In every way he was better for her than Seth Blackstone, no matter the size of Seth's…trust fund.

"That idea Angela had, about the Come to Your Senses holiday promotional? I can pay your share of the group advertising." He shrugged. "No wrapping or ribbon, but I thought you might like that."

She put the pink rose back into its bucket, incredibly touched, and yes, feeling guilty for assuming Seth had been about to bribe her with some expensive gift. Instead, he was trying to help out, knowing she struggled to keep up with expenses others could take on without blinking. "Seth. That is so sweet. But I can't let you—"

"Hey, this is a present." He gave her a severe look, which made him so fiercely sexy she wanted to attack him. But, being newly-in-control Bonnie, she didn't. "Very rude to turn it down."

"How about a loan?"

"How about a gift?"

"How about half of the cost?"

"How about all of the cost?" He put a finger to her lips as she was about to speak again. She tried very hard not to shiver, and nearly succeeded. "Look, Bonnie, I have unfair amounts of money, you're struggling right now, this would make me happy, and it would make it possible for you to be part of the Come to Your Senses special, which you should be because it makes brilliant business sense. So stuff the pride down your pants and say, 'Seth, you utterly astounding man, I bow to your mind-blowing brilliance and accept.'"

Bonnie bit her lip, thinking it over. If the group did a lot of advertising, which they should, the costs would probably add up to the total of what she had in her savings account. A loan would help. An outright gift would help even more. Seth had offered financial assistance several times and she'd always turned him down, but she did desperately want to be part of the event. "How about a simple thank-you?"

"Hmm." He pretended to consider. "So a blow job is out of the question?"

"Seth!" She cracked up, knowing he was kidding, pushing away the image of that incredibly sexy look he got on his face when she— "It is most definitely out of the question."

"Okay, okay." He grinned, which turned him instantly from bad boy to farm boy, a transition that never stopped amazing her. "I'm glad you'll let me help."

"I'm really grateful, Seth. You know I am."

"Yeah…" He dropped his head and rubbed the back of his neck, which meant he had something emotionally risky or otherwise difficult to say. "So you seeing that Don guy again?"

"I am." Sadness started building in her chest just when she most wanted to feel happy. She turned away, moved to a bucket of gerbera daisies, unable to face him. "We're going out to dinner tonight."

"That's fast. Didn't you just have a first date with him?"

"Fast?" She glanced at him over her shoulder. "You and I were in bed within a week."

"Geez, Bon." His voice was tight. "You're going to sleep with him?"

Bonnie's throat cramped. Ironic that she so hated causing him pain, since he'd caused her so damn much so many times.

"Seth." She turned to find he'd come up behind her much closer than she expected. With buckets at her back, she couldn't move away, had to tip her head to meet his gray eyes, which showed a flash of entirely uncharacteristic vulnerability. "I am a grown woman who has met a man I really like. If I continue to really like him then yes. Sleeping together is a natural progression."

The second the words were out of her mouth she regretted them. No, not quite regretted. She'd spoken the truth. But this was Seth. A man she cared for...*had* cared for very, very much. And the way his beautiful tough-guy eyes had just gone dead and his strong jaw had turned to stone, she knew she was hurting him. But since, in his typically caveman way, he was having trouble accepting the idea of Bonnie with someone else, she might as well be blunt, even if it seemed cruel.

And frankly, she'd spent the better part of the past nearly two years since moving into this building watching Seth parade around with one stunning woman after another, so she couldn't say she was totally dying of sympathy. Maybe now he'd start cluing into what her life had been like so many times after he left her. Not that she'd ever want to be vindictive about this. Just pay him back a little. Which was different. Sort of.

"I was wondering." He had his hands in his pockets and was looking down at her with that magnetic gaze that used to regularly set her on fire. "If you wanted to have dinner sometime. Maybe Friday? Either out or at my place?"

She gaped at him, heat flooding her face. Never in the five years since they'd broken up had he ever issued an advance invitation like this, as if he was asking her on a formal date. In fact, not even while they were dating. Their plans were always made last-minute. Hey, let's do this, let's do that, here's what I feel like, how about you?

"Wow. Seth, that is really sweet. And you are the world's greatest cook. I just don't think it's a good idea."

"Why?" He put his hands on his hips, which seemed to broaden his chest, make his proximity even more intimate. "Did you and Don agree not to see other people?"

"No, no." She laughed nervously. "A little too soon for that."

"So you're open to dating other men?"

"Well, yes, but, Seth—"

"Am I not a man?" He glanced down at his pants suspiciously. "I'm pretty sure I qualify."

Did he ever. "Seth, come on. It's different with you and me."

"How about if it wasn't?"

She frowned at him. "What do you mean?"

He took a deep breath, clearly struggling. "How about if we erased everything and started over? You and me. A first date."

She narrowed her eyes. What was this about? He'd told her a couple of months ago that he was starting therapy, to learn why he was resisting her. Had his invitation evolved from that process?

"I'm sorry, Seth, I don't think that would be a good idea."

"You afraid?" His eyebrow quirked; he was already

gaining confidence, knowing how much she hated that particular taunt.

"Of *you?*" She threw out a loud and unconvincing "Ha!"

"Prove it. Have dinner with me." He was too close, the pull of his body undeniable. "Upstairs, my place, Friday night."

He was right. She was afraid. Terribly afraid. Afraid of falling for him again. Afraid of being hurt. She'd come such a long way, had worked so hard to be at peace around him. No way was she going back to vulnerability and pain. He and his therapist might like the idea of starting over, but you couldn't chuck as much baggage as they had just by wanting to.

"Sorry, can't."

"You mean won't?"

Bonnie nodded brusquely, lump the size of Cleveland in her throat, wanting to have dinner with him, hating that she did and that he was making her choose yet again. "Won't."

"I was planning to make shepherd's pie. With chocolate hazelnut cheesecake for dessert."

She glared at him. "You like to fight dirty."

"Seven o'clock?"

"I'm not coming."

"Think about it."

She rolled her eyes. When he got like this, he wouldn't let go. Probably because he sensed her hesitation, sensed her slight weakness. Seth knew her way, way too well, and having grown up extremely wealthy, he was used to getting what he wanted. Though his parents had skimped on the things that really mattered, like love and attention. "I won't change my mind."

She saw the triumph in his eyes. He thought he had her.

If he was talking about the chocolate hazelnut cheese-cake, he might be right as far as her appetite went. The rest of her? He couldn't have that. She was keeping that safe. Safe for a new man and for herself.

TEARS RAN DOWN Demi's cheeks, which she bravely ignored. She and Wesley were sitting at her kitchen table shoveling in mouthfuls of the incendiary Noodles from Hell from their favorite Thai restaurant. They both adored and suffered through the dish, though they considered it a badge of honor not to wince or admit to the chili-induced agony. Demi had bought Wesley his drink at Joe Bar, and they'd come back here for dinner and dessert, in the mood for some edible torture.

"So tell me something." Demi cheated just a little by pushing aside a particularly large chunk of red bird's-eye chili pepper. Big difference between brave and suicidal. "Why is it that men are considered strong if they don't show emotion? Who decided that was masculine?"

"Hmm." Wesley stifled a gasp and poured half a beer down his throat. "If I had to answer that…"

"Which you do because I asked."

"I'd say because children have no control over emotions and women have less control than men. Women and children are weak and need protecting—" He held up his hand to stop Demi's outrage. "Calm down, I'm speaking biologically."

"Okay…" She grudgingly let him continue.

"So in order to be least like women and children—in other words, the most masculine—men have to be strong and emotionless."

"Doesn't that seem stupid to you?"

"Extremely." He ate another mouthful, chewing cautiously. "If it was up to me, we'd change it. But for some reason it isn't."

Demi frowned at him, thinking he looked better and

stronger every time she saw him. "We need to put you in charge, Wesley. Of the globe. Would you mind?"

His blue eyes went wide. "Could I still have ice cream?"

"Absolutely." She took a sip of beer and pushed her plate away, tired of her dinner giving her first-degree burns. "How did you escape the Culture of Macho?"

"I wouldn't say I escaped." He rubbed a hand thoughtfully through his thick, dark hair. "Though I did cry during one of our appointments."

"I remember." She reached to squeeze his hand. "Nearly broke my heart."

"Softie."

"Me? I'm hard as nails. But we were talking about you."

"As we should be." He smiled his easy, dynamite smile. "I had three sisters, for one. And my dad was emotional. He was also crazy about my mom and we got to see that. He cried when he was really sad, and acted as if that was completely normal."

"Which it is."

"He helped around the house in nontraditional ways, too."

"My dad didn't do squat. My sister-in-law is finding out what that's like, too, since my brother takes after him." She gestured to Wesley with her beer. "Your wife will be one lucky woman."

"So will your husband." He laughed at the sight of her startled face. "Scared you, huh."

"Husband? *Husband?*" She clutched at her chest. "I'm too young. Husbands are for grown-ups."

"In some cultures twenty-eight would make you a hopeless spinster."

"I'd make a good one."

"No, you wouldn't, Demi." His dark-lashed eyes took on

a warmth that made her blush. "Too much passion in you to waste on sexual aids."

"Oh, geez." She made a hideous face, hiding giggles.

"So…" He spoke so casually she went on instant alert. "Demi…"

"Wesley…?"

"What brought up all this talk about the Culture of Macho and marriage?" He put a long finger to his cheek and tipped his head. "Could it have anything to do with yesterday's visit by Colin 'Ironman' Russo?"

"Of course it does. Well, no, not the marriage part." She gave an exaggerated shudder. "But the guy can barely move. I worked really deeply on him and he does this whole stoic statue thing. It just seems stupid he couldn't yell, 'Ow, that effing hurts!'"

Wesley looked at her skeptically. "Would *you* do that in a professional office?"

"Nope," she said cheerfully. "That's partly my point, too. It's ridiculous for anyone to hide normal feelings of pain."

"Your studio would get kind of noisy."

"At times." She twisted her mouth, pushing her unused knife back and forth on the tablecloth. "Truth is, I'm not sure what to do about him."

"Jump him?"

She wasn't going to dignify that with a response. "He's not only hurting in his body."

"I'm not surprised." Wesley drained his beer, his handsome face shadowed. "Tough journey out of that pain."

"He wasn't hurt nearly as badly as you were, but like you his athletic career meant everything to him."

"He just thinks it does."

"Yes, he just thinks it does. That's my point. You found coaching. I'm not sure what he'll do." She swirled more pasta onto her fork, mouth craving another shot of pain. "I wonder if he should meet you and hear about—"

"Ha!" Wesley was already shaking his head. "Hear about my sad story? So you can say hey, guess what? Instead of being a world champion triathlete, you could be a suburban high-school track coach. He's not ready for that."

"He might be."

Wesley gave her a look.

"At some point he might be," Demi said.

"Then at some point I'd be happy to."

"He'll get there. I just need to make sure I don't push him too hard." She laughed. "I mean emotionally. I don't think I *can* push him too hard physically. He'd work until both legs dropped off and barely notice."

"Exercise addicts are like that."

"Exactly." Demi stood and carried their plates to her sink, surprised at how rattled she felt by this discussion. "Want some ice cream?"

"Is there any answer possible besides yes?"

"Nope." She opened the freezer. "Häagen-Dazs Vanilla Swiss Almond?"

Wesley groaned. "Do you know what it's like having to cut back from a three-thousand-calorie diet?"

"Nope." She pried the top off the carton. "One scoop or two?"

"Two." He sighed resignedly and patted his flat stomach. "Already gained ten pounds, what's a couple more?"

"Yeah, but you were down way low from running, Wesley. You look great." She tried not to compare his lean, slender frame to the broad torso and hard muscles of her triathlete obsession. She should picture Colin hugely obese.

That didn't work, either.

"What does this god among men do besides work out?"

Demi served him a glare along with his ice cream and

a spoon. "He used to play sax and he made knives from scratch before he became a triathlon junkie. Maybe he can go back to that."

Wesley's silence made her look up from scooping her own ice cream. He was staring at her, shaking his head. "Strange."

"What is?"

"I don't ever remember you talking about a client so much."

Blush. Inevitable. Unwelcome. *Grrr.* "He's an interesting case."

"Uh…ruptured disc? Dime a dozen."

"No, but I mean…" What did she mean? She sat down and lost herself in her first bite of Häagen-Dazs heaven instead of trying to figure it out.

"What else could be unusual?" He pretended to count on his fingers. "Had to give up an athletic career, I think you've seen that before. Trouble adjusting to new reality of his body, ditto…"

"Yes. I know, but—"

"Me?" He put his counting fingers away and dived into his dessert again. "I think you're hot for this guy."

"No. No way. No. That is ridiculous. Completely—" She broke off, wrinkling her nose. "I'm objecting too much, aren't I."

"You said it, not me."

"Okay, okay." She licked her spoon and heaped up another bite, making sure it had plenty of chocolate-covered almonds in it. "He's hot. So what?"

"So what are you going to do?"

"Do? I'm going to help his pain, teach him how to manage the injury, try to show him that his life isn't over and wish him well. What did you think?"

"I don't know, ask him out?"

"A client? Don't think so."

"We went out."

"You asked me. *After* we finished working together."

"Make his treatment short, then ask him out. Or I know." He brightened. "Send him to a friend. What about whatsername, Julie, who you used to—"

"He came to me, I'm his physical therapist and I will treat him."

"Ooh." Wesley narrowed his eyes. "Mighty possessive, aren't we."

"Professional. Why are you so anxious to foist me off on this poor man?"

He reached across the table and ruffled her hair, chuckling. "Because I know you well enough to know that the more you like a guy—if the way you acted with me was any indication—the colder and more professional you become. So he probably has no idea that you're leaving drool spots on his blanket."

"Am not." She gave him a sidelong glance. "Okay, that one was a mistake."

Wesley cracked up. "Okay, okay. But I'm right. So think about it."

"Yes, master." He was right about the way she acted around guys she was attracted to. In high school, for four long years she'd been passionately in puppy love with Brad Johnston. Time after time she'd been in situations where she could have gotten to know him. School paper. School plays. Social-activity committee meetings. But the more she adored him, the less she spoke to him. So guess what, they never went out. Someday she was going to run across him, grab him and plant on him that kiss she'd fantasized about every night. The guy would have no idea what had happened. He probably didn't even remember her.

However, in this case, her shyness was a good thing. If

Colin caught wind of her attraction he could cause unpleasantness that would damage her professional reputation.

"In any case, I'm mostly interested in helping him."

"I know. That's what I love about you." Wesley let his spoon fall back into his bowl and heaved himself out of the chair, something he couldn't have done that well even six months earlier. "I should go. This was fabulous, thanks. Need help with the dishes?"

"Nah. They all go in the dishwasher."

She gave him a hug, congratulated him again on his successful second date with Cathy the previous evening and sent him shuffling off. His balance was much improved from when she'd started working with him two years earlier, but his gait was still not the graceful stride he must have had before the accident. She hoped Cathy fell madly in love with him. Hell, she wished *she* could have fallen madly in love with him. But Demi too often seemed to go for men who wouldn't look twice at her. Sometimes she thought she was sabotaging herself. Other times she figured it was because she essentially made herself invisible around the guys she wanted.

Love and relationships were so confusing, sometimes she wished she didn't want either one.

She carried the ice-cream bowls to the sink, rinsed and stuck all the dishes in the dishwasher, then curled up in her favorite recliner with her knitting and the audiobook she'd been making piss-poor progress on in the past few days ready to play on her iPod. Great story about a guy who thought he—

Phone.

She sighed and put down her knitting. She looked at the display and sighed again, louder. Carrie, her sister. Demi wasn't in the mood. But if she didn't answer now, Carrie would call back and leave increasingly hysterical messages about how she was starting to picture Demi lying dead in her apartment. Carrie never used to be *that* neurotic, but in the past few months she'd gotten more clingy and more intensely…herself.

"Hi, Carrie."

"Hey, little sister. How's everything?"

"Good." She braced herself. Of course she'd have to ask the question back, only her sister wouldn't be able to answer in one syllable. She'd need at least a hundred. And all her "problems" would be these amazingly impressive ones that made Demi feel like cow poo. "How about you?"

"Crazy, crazy busy. Dan got another promotion, which means he's traveling nearly the entire week every week, and keeps missing the kids' school stuff. Rachel got the lead in their second-grade play, and Boris started the Suzuki violin program at his preschool. I'm actually busy selling houses, which I can't believe, considering how strange the market has been."

So strange she had to give up one of her twice-weekly massage appointments. "I'm glad to hear that."

"Oh, and guess what? My black-forest cake took first place twice at our Oktoberfest celebration! Once for taste and once for appearance. I tweaked Mom's recipe, and then I made the cake in the shape of a Bollenhut!"

"A what?"

"The traditional Black Forest hat." As if Demi should know that, as if everyone else on the planet did and what was wrong with her?

More to the point, what was wrong with Carrie? It was as if she'd gotten stuck in her highest gear. In a normal family, Demi would simply ask what was bugging her. But her family wasn't normal; they didn't discuss emotions. "That is fabulous, Carrie. Congratulations."

"Aw, thanks. So tell me more of what's going on with you?"

Demi closed her eyes wearily. This happened every time. What was Demi doing? Not being promoted, not raising overachieving kids, not baking prizewinning from-scratch cakes. "Same ol' same ol'. Working, hanging out."

"You dating anyone?"

"Not right now, no."

"Are you *trying* to date anyone?"

"Not really."

"Why?" Carrie was clearly aghast. Their parents had married in their teens, as had Carrie and their brother, Mike. Once again Demi was struck by the amazing irony that Carrie and Mike, the children her mom and dad adopted when they thought they couldn't have children themselves, were much more like them than Demi, the "surprise!" daughter they had conceived naturally a few years later.

"I don't know, Carrie. If I meet someone I'm not against starting something, but—"

"What about online dating?"

She made a face. After what Bonnie had gone through, the idea appealed not at all. The concept of structuring her life around achieving or failing to have a relationship bothered her, too. "I'm sure I'll meet someone when the time is right."

"You have to go after what you want, Demi."

"Yes." She spoke tightly. Going after what you wanted was a lot easier when you were endowed with beauty, strong extroversion and an unshakable self-confidence. Demi had done just fine considering she had none of those. "I always have. But what you want isn't necessarily what—"

"You don't want to be happy?"

Demi indulged in her most exasperated face for a good three seconds, wishing she had a mirror since she was pretty sure this was one of her best ever. She had plenty of experience making them while talking to her sister. "Of course I want to be happy. It's just that what makes you happy isn't what—"

"Hang on, doorbell. Rachel's being dropped off. Can I call you back?"

No. "Um, I'm about to go to bed."

"Bed *now?*"

"Yeah, long day." She faked a yawn that was pretty good if she said so herself.

"Oh. Okay. *Coming.* Listen, I gotta go."

"Sure, Carrie. Talk to you later. Thanks for calling."

She hung up the phone, found herself clenching her abdominal wall, and pretty much every muscle in her neck and shoulders, and forced herself to relax.

You don't want to be happy?

Honestly. No, she wanted to spend the rest of her life as miserable as possible. Which she would be if she tried to do anything her sister recommended.

Except maybe dating. Maybe. But every time Demi thought of signing up for a dating site, putting herself out there to be judged, found lacking, found appropriate, found whatever…ugh. Bonnie had the motivation and the stamina for that experience. Demi was pretty sure it would either make her crazy or crush her.

But her reaction to her sister's suggestion—the anger, the impatience— She hadn't majored in psychology for nothing. Carrie had hit a nerve.

Okay. Demi would look honestly inside herself and ask the magic question.

Why wasn't she dating?

She was twenty-eight and did want to marry and have children. But there weren't any men she was even attracted to…

Oh, great. One possibility popped into her head with such speed it startled her, though given Wesley's recent teasing it shouldn't have, and just as quickly made her laugh. Right. Good idea. Complete pipe dream even if he was single, and if that wasn't enough, add unethical and—gorgeous male body notwithstanding—not an appealing personality.

Colin Russo, cranky ex-jock with abs of steel and a crappy attitude.

Only in her dreams.

4

DEMI ANDERSON HAD the greatest hands in Seattle. Colin would argue with anyone on that point. He was lying on her massage table, that horrible music playing, candles lit. The usual spicy too-rich smell of whatever she was spraying in the room mixed unpleasantly with the peppermint oil she rubbed all over him.

It was just that the rubbed-all-over-him part was really, really good.

She'd been right that he'd be sore after their first session. He'd woken up the next morning feeling as if he'd been beaten up by a gang. But she was also right that his muscles would loosen, and after she'd worked on him deeply again last week, things were getting better. He still felt like an old man, but at least he had hopes of becoming young again.

Her hands moved down to his lower back. Colin suppressed a groan of pleasure. They'd mostly done exercises today, but Demi always finished sessions with a brief massage.

Fine by him.

Her hands were strong, supple. She hit the perfect balance between keeping her touch clinical and making him feel as if she was touching him because she enjoyed it.

Now that he wasn't in so much pain, he *definitely* enjoyed it.

Her hands continued down, following the path of his gluteals.

This time he couldn't keep the groan silent.

"You okay?"

"Fine." He spoke abruptly so as not to betray what was happening to his body. Five times six was thirty. Five times seven, thirty-five. Five times…um…

Her hands slowed, dug in deeper, kneading the muscle. Eight times nine, uh…was seventy…something.

Oh, man.

The pain in his back might have eased but he was going to be experiencing quite a bit in a different place if he didn't stop thinking about where she was touching—

"Turn over for me?"

"Uh…" Colin tensed, which was the last thing he wanted to do. Demi had never asked him to turn before. "I can't right now."

She made a sound of concern. "Where is the pain?"

How the hell was he supposed to answer that? *Between my legs* would be the most honest. *As if I'm lying on a tree root.* But he wasn't going there. "Give me a minute."

"If you tell me where—"

"It's fine now." His annoyance and embarrassment were already minimizing the problem, but he still moved slowly, glancing at Demi, who was frowning worriedly. "You just had me in an, uh, altered state."

Her face relaxed; she nodded, then pushed a strand of hair behind her ear and held it there for a second, as if hoping it would stick with enough pressure. She wore black today, as always. The color brought out her hair and brows and made her pale skin paler except for her mouth, which was a soft rose color. A full, sensual mouth. "It's good that you can disappear into the massage. I think the more you can leave yourself the better."

"Yeah." Leave himself? What did she mean by that? It made no sense that he was still attracted to her. The first day or two, okay, but by now…they had less than nothing in common.

"So how about…" She gestured for him to lie down.

"Uh. I'm actually done for today." No way in hell was he lying on his back with a sheet over him. *Demi, if you've ever wanted to see a pyramid, today's your lucky day.*

"Done?" She looked surprised, then shifted her features into neutral. "Sure. See you in my office. Take your time getting up."

"Right." Getting up wasn't the problem.

He dressed, pleased to be able to step into his jeans and pull them up in less than a minute, which was still a hell of a long time when it came to pants, but better than it used to be. Baby steps for old man Colin.

No, he hadn't lost his impatience, but he had to say that being in the calm, capable hands of Demi, forcing himself to accept her treatment plan, being able finally to hear and understand the stages of recovery he still had ahead of him—yeah, he was doing better.

If only he could stop thinking about her. While he was at home exercising, he was imagining her encouragement, her corrections, her concern. While he was walking in his neighborhood or in a nearby park, he heard her voice correcting his posture, urging him to be patient, not to extend himself too far. He felt as if she were personally invested in his journey back to health. Even knowing that acting that way was part of her job, Colin couldn't help responding. She had a rare gift.

Yeah, so did he: for feeling sorry for himself. If nothing else, Demi was helping to get him out of that rut bit by bit. He should know better, being a competitor. Negativity helped nothing, could sap all chance of accomplishing goals. Slowly, he was absorbing her trinity: positive thinking, can-do attitudes and silver linings.

He left the small room, which had seemed oddly diminished by Demi's absence, and sauntered over to her office, where he'd left his sax earlier, looking forward to their postsession consultation. He had a growing and unwelcome need to get behind her calm, professional exterior and discover what she was hiding.

Crazy talk. He needed to get out more. He should throw his stupid pride and pain under a bus and meet with Nick and their training group sometime for a drink. Or two. He should call Stephanie and pretend he was just wondering how she was, testing the waters for their eventual reconciliation. Anything but fixating on some schoolboy thing he had for his PT.

In Demi's office, he sat in his usual chair, careful not to slouch or she'd get on him about "stacking his vertebrae." He felt sorry for whomever she married. The guy would have the posture of a ballet dancer or get nagged to death.

"You seem better, that accurate? Both in body and attitude?" She turned a page, seemingly absorbed in some report. The woman sure loved her paperwork.

"If that's what the sacred file says, it must be true."

She rolled her eyes. "What do *you* say, Colin?"

"I say yeah." He couldn't help a smile. "I am doing better, thank you for asking, Ms. Anderson."

"Honestly." Demi bent down and retrieved his sax, passed it across the top of her desk as if she was handing him a revolver for their next round of Russian roulette. "Show me."

He opened the case and hauled out the instrument, put it together, stupidly nervous. He wasn't auditioning for Duke

Ellington here, just making sure he could play the thing without hurting himself. Last night he'd perversely resisted practicing to prove he wasn't out to impress Demi, so he hadn't touched the sax in years. She'd have to deal with that.

Taking the reed, he stuck it in his mouth, wetting it to vibrate properly. The taste and feel of the slender wood piece brought back countless memories, from serenading Stephanie to avoiding his father's disapproval by practicing in the basement of his childhood home, pretending to be John Coltrane or Charlie Parker.

He fitted the wet reed into the mouthpiece, tightened it in place, put the strap over his head and stood, adjusting the instrument's neck until its angle suited him. The sax felt good against him again, familiar in his hands, like a reunion with an old, true companion. Though it remained to be seen how the quality of their friendship had withstood the separation…

"Here goes." He closed his eyes, running his fingers over the keys, hearing the tune in his head before he played.

When Sunny gets blue…

The instrument squawked, then again, but after the first phrase Colin got the feel back in his mouth and hands, got into the music. No, he wasn't Charlie Parker, would never come close, but playing felt damn good. Demi didn't stop him, and once he started playing, really playing, he didn't want to stop himself, either. He blew the melody slowly and simply, then repeated it with flourishes and embellishments, jazzy, soulful, whatever came to him.

But of course he had to stop eventually. The last note faded; he opened his eyes, letting the sound fade from his mind as well, then turned to Demi.

She was watching him, color high in that pale Snow White face with the rosy lips and dented chin. For a crazy few seconds their eyes held, and something deeper than their gazes connected. Emotions flooded Colin's brain and heart, like the deluge ending to a long dry season. Then Demi blinked and looked down at her beloved files, her refuge, and he slowly took the instrument off his neck, still in some kind of weird music—and Demi—induced trance.

When she looked back up it was all business again; the flood receded abruptly.

"That was really good, Colin. You have real musical talent."

"Yeah, thanks." Her goal was to rebuild his self-esteem, make him think about something other than being a failed triathlete. She'd compliment him no matter how he played. What annoyed him was that he found himself wishing he knew if she meant the words sincerely. Why would he care what his PT thought of his playing? He played first and foremost for himself. Always had.

"You're holding the instrument fine. I'm guessing that you have to keep good posture in order to breathe well. Just make sure you don't sway around too much yet. Otherwise great."

"Okay." He packed up his saxophone and glanced at the clock, shocked to realize how long he'd been playing. "I went over our time."

"No problem. I'm taking lunch now."

"Then I cut your lunch short." He closed the lid of the case, even more annoyed now. Holding the instrument in his hands again had fed something he hadn't realized was hungry. He didn't have any right to involve Demi's personal time in his epiphanies. "Where do you eat?"

"I bring a lunch or buy takeout and eat at Cal Anderson Park." She spoke matter-of-factly, but blushed. She was fine putting her hands all over his body, but admitting she ate alone in the park embarrassed her? It didn't embarrass him.

It made him feel protective of her. He scoffed at himself. What, like she was a baby rabbit or something? *Come on.*

"I'll get going, then." He thanked her for the session and strode out into the hallway, pausing outside Bonnie Blooms, idly imagining Demi with a blossom pinned into her hair.

With a what? *Blossom?* What the hell was wrong with him?

Lunchtime. He needed food. But at his condo right now there was only peanut butter, cheese, pickles, emptiness and boredom. He pushed out of the building and stood on the front steps for a minute or two, breathing in the soft, fresh air. A beautiful, warm fall day—in the mid-sixties, he'd guess. Eating outdoors wasn't a bad idea.

The door opened behind him. Demi came through, saw him and stopped in her tracks. He reached to hold the door over her head before it hit her.

"Oh. Hi." She was clearly as caught off guard as he was.

Colin responded with a nod, let go of the door after she moved through. Out here, away from her territory, they weren't client and physical therapist anymore. What were they? Not strangers. Not friends.

"So…are you meeting someone?" she asked.

"Nope." He saw the question in her eyes. *Then why are you standing alone on the steps?* "Just indecisive. What's good to eat around here?"

"You like hot dogs?"

She surprised him. He'd expected her to name some vegan place where he could get tofu twenty-four ways. Fine by him, he loved tofu. But he also loved hot dogs, though he hardly ever ate them because they were loaded with God knew what, and like most athletes, he put into his body what he wanted to get out of it. Feed your body crap, it performs like crap. Right now, however, a big, juicy dog sounded like heaven. "Bring 'em on."

"How do you like them?" She quirked an eyebrow at him. Clearly this was a test. "Loaded or un-?"

"Loaded, baby."

"Ah." She pointed down Broadway, obviously approving of his choice. "There's a cart near the park that sells big natural-casing dogs, the kind that explode juice in your mouth when you bite. Awesome white bakery buns, not too fluffy but not heavy. And the toppings…"

Her eyes were bright, and a small smile curved her mouth as she spoke, gesturing with her hands. By the time she got to "toppings," she was practically sighing in ecstasy. Colin was fascinated and mildly aroused. Demi Anderson turned sexual over hot dogs. Intriguing. "They're that good?"

"Chili; sauerkraut; jalapeños; onions, grilled or fresh; mustard, yellow, brown or Dijon; ketchup; barbecue sauce; shredded cheddar; cream cheese; pickles; coleslaw—you can have pretty much anything."

"Oh, man, I'm dying." He put a hand to his rumbling stomach. "Is that what you're eating?"

Her features froze, as if she'd been caught in an unexpected trap. She nodded stiffly. "Yup."

"You want some company?"

Demi blinked twice, her color deepening. The blush was cute, softened her further, made him feel big-brother protective. No, not brother. More like her big brother's best friend. Who'd discovered his buddy's little sister had done some growing up.

Crazy. Women with spirit attracted him, women who challenged him. Stephanie had done that constantly, sometimes with shows of temper or hysteria that Colin had learned to roll his eyes at and tolerate. She always calmed down.

"I don't— I can't be with— You're a client."

"And?" He set his jaw. He hadn't asked her to sleep with him, just eat a freaking hot dog.

"I'm not…" She took a deep breath, pushed hair behind her ear. Colin waited, but she was clearly too flustered to explain further.

"Okay. Not a big deal. I'll see you next week." He went down the steps, more annoyed than he should be. She had her code of ethics, this crossed it for whatever reason. He didn't have to pout as if she'd rejected him personally. He'd buy his own damn hot dog and they could eat on opposite sides of the park.

"Colin."

He turned. Demi still stood at the top of the steps wearing a determined expression. "Lunch would be nice. Thank you."

Unexpected pleasure. He found himself smiling somewhat goofily. "Well, good."

"Okay, then." She smiled, too, then laughed. First time he'd seen her let loose even halfway, and it nearly blew him over. From mousy mystery to a vibrant, magnetic woman.

"Hot dogs." He gestured toward Broadway, feeling unaccountably giddy. "Let's go."

They walked down the street, somewhat predictably discussing the nice weather, until they passed a shop window and he realized he'd lost Demi to the pull of whatever was in it.

Edwin's Jewelers. Another surprise. He'd never noticed her wearing jewelry, though now that he looked she did have on small silver earrings in the shape of some flower.

"Look at that." She pointed when he came up beside her and he followed her finger. Draped around one of those weird headless models was a necklace of twisted silver that grew into a delicate floral vine studded with diamonds. "Isn't that gorgeous?"

"You going to buy it?" he teased.

"I've got nearly a dozen."

Colin's eyes shot wide. The piece would sell for thousands. "You've bought a dozen—"

"No, no, I don't buy them. I collect them." She tapped her head and smiled self-consciously. "Mentally. It's a game Mom started when I was a little girl. She or my sister would see something one of them liked and we'd pretend we were going to buy it."

He squinted at the necklace, trying to imagine her and a dark-haired sister holding their mother's hand, ogling jewelry. He'd sort of pictured Demi as a tomboy. "Wait, didn't *you* ever see anything you wanted?"

"Not usually." She spoke matter-of-factly, still staring at the piece on the decapitated model. "I wasn't that into jewelry or most of the girlie things Mom and Carrie enjoyed. Sometimes I felt as if I came from a different planet than the rest of my family."

"That's tough to handle." He felt sudden strong empathy. Boy did he know what that was like.

"Anyway. It's a silly game. Not sure why I still play it."

"Because it's fun?"

"It is and it isn't." She grinned wryly. "Not so great to spend time focusing on what you can't have. Know what I mean?"

He sent her a look. "Is this going to be lunch or more can-do therapy?"

"Lunch. I promise." She gave the necklace one more look before moving away. His picture of her with the flower in her hair zoomed back for a wider shot; now diamonds sparkled against her skin. Because she was wearing a dress with a plunging V that was…very nice.

"Did your parents play games like that with you?" She ambled along and he found himself liking the feel of her next to him, liking the way she moved and the way their shoulders bumped occasionally.

He was really losing it.

"My parents weren't much for games. Dad was a pretty serious guy. Mom did whatever he wanted."

"No good strong female role models for you, then?"

He hadn't thought about it that way. "I don't know. I had a kick-ass female sax teacher. She'd been everywhere, done everything. Used to let me drink beer after lessons."

"Underage?"

"Yeah. Betty Sandison. I thought she was the coolest thing ever."

"Betty Sandison is not a beer-drinking name. I'm thinking aprons with ducks on them and meat-loaf dinners."

"Definitely not this Betty."

"Is your girlfriend more like your mom or like her?"

Colin gritted his teeth. He did not want to talk about Stephanie with anyone and especially not with Demi and double-especially not now. "What's with all the questions?"

"What's with the fear of answering?"

He stopped on the sidewalk, faced her with hands on his hips. She had him off balance and he didn't like that, wasn't used to it. "I am not afraid of answering."

"Good to know." She broke into that surprise smile and pointed left on Howell Street. "Hot-dog cart is at the end of this block."

He followed her, wondering if she'd agreed to have lunch with him in a purely professional capacity for the purpose of digging deeper into his psyche, and then wondering why that bothered him.

Too much bleeping wondering. When his body was static like this it left his mind too much to do.

Happily, within a few minutes, his mind was busy choosing toppings for his dogs. Sauerkraut, mustard and jalapeños on one. Chili and cheese on the other. Demi ordered hers with coleslaw and pickle, a combination Colin reminded himself to try next time. Chips and drinks next, then he pulled out his wallet to pay the weathered guy manning the cart.

So did Demi.

"Let me buy you a hot dog."

"No, no." She shook her head and fumbled for bills. "I'll pay mine, you pay yours."

"Forget it." He shoved a ten at the vendor, having expected her reaction. "It's a few bucks. You can deduct it from your bill if it's that important."

"Well…" She frowned, bunching her rosy mouth. "Thank you."

"You're welcome." He picked up the bag, pleased she'd let him win that one.

The Howell Street entrance brought them into Cal Anderson Park by the cone-shaped fountain, its waters flowing into a long stone channel that emptied into a rectangular pool. Two women were just leaving one of the benches by the pool. Colin and Demi quickened their steps and grabbed it, beating out a couple of suited businessmen by seconds.

"Big score," Demi said. "These benches are never available, even in winter."

"You sit out here all year?"

"Unless it's really cold or really hot." She took the hot dog, drink and chips he handed her. "I like being outdoors."

"You like being alone?"

"Don't mind it." She unwrapped her dog. "It's my nature. My parents, brother and sister need people around all the time. That would exhaust me."

"I'm in between." He took a bite of his chili dog. Spicy, juicy, hot—she was right. This was a superior fat-and-salt vehicle. "Oh, man, these are good."

"Told you."

"You did." He grinned at her. "Thanks."

She ducked her head, took a bite of her own dog, retrieving cabbage strands that tried to stay in the bun. A blob of coleslaw fell onto her lap. She picked it off and absently brushed at the spot with her napkin.

Colin grinned. Stephanie would have had a fit about her clumsiness and potential dry-cleaning bills. He liked that Demi didn't even seem to notice. "So what do you do besides heal people and collect virtual jewelry?"

"Oh." The question seemed to take her aback. "Well. I read. I knit. And I run."

He waited. Was that it? No parties, movie outings, dinners, clubs, classes… He felt that same weird jolt of protective concern. A woman like Demi shouldn't waste herself being alone. "Not a partyer, huh."

"Nope."

"Friends?"

She gave him a look. "No. None at all. I hate people."

"Right." Touché. But again he liked that she wasn't apologetic. Most of his friends indulged in competitive bragging over how much excitement they could cram into their lives. Her attitude was refreshing. Books, yarn and running, there it was. Unfortunately, his reading was sketchy, though he'd been doing more since his injury, and he had zero questions to ask about knitting. "How far do you run?"

"Five miles some days, three others." She crunched on a chip and licked a crumb off her finger. "Depends on my energy level and time."

"Do you lift?" He was suddenly having to work hard at focusing on what she was saying instead of imagining her naked. She was slender, tall, probably five foot eight or nine, and her fitness routine meant she must be well muscled under all that black clothing. Plus her tongue looked very hot licking her finger.

He was such a guy.

"Free weights. Just to stay strong. Nothing obsessive. I use muscle at work."

"I've felt that." He finished his chili dog, started in on the kraut and jalapeño combo, glad he wasn't planning to kiss anyone that night.

Which immediately had him wondering what it would be like to kiss Demi. Her mouth was nicely shaped, with wide, curling corners and a full, lush center. Appealing. Sexy even.

Very sexy.

Okay. He wanted her. For whatever reason. He did. Rather badly. First woman in a long time besides Stephanie—whom he'd wanted beyond reason from the second he'd laid eyes on her.

Demi wouldn't want him back. If she had this much trouble having lunch with him, she wouldn't jump on an invitation to…jump on him.

But he was single. And if reading and knitting filled the bulk of her free time, he'd bet she was, too.

Hmm…

"You seeing anyone, Demi?"

"Nope." She said the word a little too loudly and a little too cheerfully. "Why?"

"I wanted to know." He turned and gazed at her directly. "For the record, Stephanie is more like Betty Sandison than my mother."

"Ah." She nodded, sending him a sidelong look from her wide dark eyes that gave him a distinctly animal reaction. Good God. There must be something in his hot dog. And why didn't he mention he wasn't seeing Stephanie anymore? They'd been together so long it felt jarring to admit. As though if he never said it, maybe it wouldn't be true.

"What do you mean, ah?"

"Ahhhh!" She opened her eyes wide, raised her brows high. "Ahhhh!"

He started chuckling, positively smitten now with this alternative version of Demi. How had this happened to him? "You've figured me out, huh."

"Oh, totally."

"Give me a break." He finished his second hot dog, opened the bag of chips. "How come you're not seeing anyone?"

She put down her drink. "That is the world's most annoying question."

"Seriously, why aren't you?"

"Because I haven't found anyone, and no one has found me, what do you think?"

He shrugged. "I don't know, maybe you're asexual."

"Ha. No, I am definitely—" She checked herself visibly. "This is not appropriate conversation."

"No?" Colin thought it was getting quite interesting. *Definitely* not asexual? Gay, maybe? He seriously doubted it.

Well. He put his arm along the back of the bench to see what she'd do. Predictably, she stiffened right up. Avoiding his touch because she didn't want it? Or because she did?

Adrenaline was flowing now. He hadn't felt this alive in quite a while.

"What would be appropriate conversation with me?"

Her cheeks were red. He liked making her blush, liked the way he could get her off balance, too. "The state of the economy. Your mental state approaching your recovery. The migration of tropical butterflies. The—"

"How about when can we have lunch again?"

She whipped her head around and looked at him as if he'd suggested they strip right there and swim naked in the fountain. "This was a one-time thing."

"Why?"

"Because I don't see clients socially."

"You're seeing me now."

"This is a one-time thing."

"Why?"

"Because you seemed to need it."

"*Need* it?" He narrowed his eyes incredulously. "A pity lunch?"

"No, not pity." She made a scornful noise, dark eyes watching him steadily. A breeze blew her hair back from her pale, pretty face. "I don't do pity."

"Then what? *Concern?*"

"Sure." Cool, professional Demi. He was starting to hate her like that. "Why is concern bad?"

He was pissed. He'd been imagining them doing very nice, very adult things together, and she'd been thinking of him as a child who needed mommying. Ego down for the count.

He crumpled his hot-dog wrapper and chip bag and stuffed them in the paper sack, held it out to Demi for her garbage. "Ready to go?"

She gave him a wary look and added her trash. "Sure."

They walked in awkward silence back to Olive Way, where Colin had parked. He shook her hand, ditching his fantasy of ending lunch with a lingering kiss on her cheek. Not likely. "'Bye. Thanks for lunch."

"Thank *you*. I'll see you next Monday."

"Right."

He got into his car. Instead of going back into the building, Demi stood on the sidewalk and watched him. What was she waiting for? What did she want? Didn't she have some other client to go feel sorry for?

Who cared? He pulled out too fast, tires screeching briefly, and was rewarded for the childish gesture and his sulky attitude with a renewed stab of pain through his back.

5

DEMI OPENED HER door, cool smile firmly in place to welcome Colin.

He wasn't there.

She stared at her watch, as if it would tell her anything different from what the clock just had. *Honestly, Demi.* The guy wasn't even late yet.

Dangerous. All morning, Demi could think of nothing but Colin showing up today. She was jittery and fizzing and distracted and for heaven's *sake.* She'd been like this all week, no matter how far she ran, no matter how earnestly she meditated, no matter how many books she read. Knitting was out of the question because it left her mind free to wander. And wander it did, over the way he'd changed into a totally different person playing the sax: sensitive, soulful and sensual. The way he'd asked her to have lunch with him, the way he'd looked so stunned after they ate when she'd hinted she'd accepted his invitation so she could get him talking, find out more about what went on in his head.

Professional curiosity had been part of the reason she'd accepted, certainly. But not all. When did a woman like Demi *ever* get a lunch invitation from a guy like Colin? A guy who could be on the cover of *Men's Health.* Or

GQ. Or *Playgirl.* Which explained why he looked shocked when she didn't jump all over him—though man, did she want to. How could someone like her be indifferent to Mr. Amazing?

She wasn't. She had to keep her guard up so high a pole vaulter couldn't get over it. No flirting. No lingering looks. No hair-flipping, eyelash-batting, luxurious stretches or drawn-out leg-uncrossing.

But Colin was so funny. And so good-looking. And so oddly charming, even when he was cranky and shut down. He'd pulled some pretty hard-to-get-at heartstrings, especially when he'd hinted that he'd grown up, as she had, trying to please unpleasable parents. Boy did Demi understand that pain and frustration.

Bottom line: she needed to stay focused and in control and…

Maybe it was just the mood he'd been in. Pretty day, lonely guy, and Demi happened to be there. Not like he'd pursue her or ask her out again.

Or maybe he would.

She closed her eyes, forcing herself to breathe in slowly, breathe out slowly. She could not, would not, give even the merest hint that she was expecting or craving anything from him. Her only goal was to serve him as best she could in a purely professional capacity.

One eye open, she peeked at the clock. He'd be waiting by now.

He wasn't.

She went back into her office, sat down and stared at his file, trying to concentrate on his treatment plan, on the nature and severity of his injury and the best way she could get him focusing on positive messages…

God he was hot. She wanted him with a fierceness that frightened her. She'd been sexually attracted to plenty of men, had indulged herself happily with a few who'd pursued her. But with Colin she wasn't following her usual pattern, wasn't putting up walls, wasn't violently tongue-tied and awkward. Well, sometimes. She was still Demi after all.

Maybe she felt more confident because he was her client, and she therefore had some authority in their interactions? Maybe. Though the more she'd found herself attracted to Wesley, the more she'd turned stony and unresponsive, and he'd been a client.

So much for that theory.

When Colin asked her to have lunch with him, her familiar self-protective instinct had quite sensibly refused, but it had been completely overpowered by such a strong longing...

Demi got up to compose herself, mildly aroused at the prospect of seeing him, of being able to touch him, smell him— Oh my goodness, she was going to have to suppress every natural impulse she had around him.

Door open.

Not there.

Sick disappointment started to settle in her stomach.

Get a grip!

She turned firmly back into her office. Okay. He wasn't coming. She could use this hour to—

The door to the waiting room burst open behind her. "Sorry I'm late."

Relief, mixed with dread, mixed with excitement, mixed with— Was there medication for this stupidity?

"No problem." She put on her best impersonal smile, which nearly fell off when she turned. Flushed as if he'd been hurrying, he was walking toward her without evident pain, wearing—God help her—tight black biking shorts and a tight blue athletic shirt, hair tousled, eyes full of life and spirit. And if he'd been sexy before...

"I rode over." The triumph on his face made her want to hug him.

"And survived." She shamelessly took the opportunity to check him out. "No pain?"

"Nope."

Uhhh. "None?"

He shrugged. "Some stiffness."

"You rode slowly?"

"Yes." He was already looking annoyed.

"Sat straight?"

"Yes."

"Walked the hills?"

"Sort of."

Demi rolled her eyes. Athletes, ptooey. "You only want to 'sort of' recover from this injury?"

His jaw set. "I walked the ones I needed to walk."

"Hmm." She gestured him into the exercise room, proud of how she was handling herself. "Let's see how much damage you've done."

After she saw him through a solid exercise session and some stretching, it turned out he'd done very little. His flexibility had improved, range of motion, too. She was really pleased for him. "Okay, time for massage. You're doing fine. But don't let this go to your head."

"Ha!" Colin stood carefully. "As if I would?"

"You would." Demi shook her head. "I can smell the testosterone from here. You're getting cocky. Be careful."

"I will." He grabbed his jacket, started rummaging in the pockets. "I'm not interested in any more setbacks."

"Good." She wiped down the mat he'd been using with alcohol and stacked it in the corner with the others, then picked up the exercise ball to find Colin holding something out for her to see. "What's that?"

"Tickets to the Earshot Jazz Festival. Saturday's concert. Full Nelson is playing."

"Oh, you're lucky. I love that band."

"They're for you. I'm giving them to you."

Oh. She put the exercise ball carefully on the rack, unsure how to respond except to say, *Are you crazy?* Why was he doing this? "Colin. That is really sweet, but I'm sorry, I can't accept—"

"Yeah, yeah, right. Take them. I don't know if my back can take sitting for that long yet."

"What about your friends?"

"They don't like jazz."

"Stephanie."

"Stephanie and I aren't seeing each other anymore."

She was startled into facing him. "I'm sorry."

"Don't bother."

Her mind went to high speed. Had he meant to go with Stephanie and couldn't face going with anyone else? What was the right thing to do in this situation? She'd accepted gifts from clients a few times, but only tokens of appreciation at their last sessions.

"No agenda, no strings. I just don't want them to go to waste." He held the tickets out insistently. "Besides, you need to get out and have fun. You can bring your knitting."

She started to get insulted, then saw the twinkle in his eyes and laughed. "One ticket for me, one for a half-finished sweater?"

"Come on. You can land a better date than that. Easy."

Like you? The image came immediately, straight out of the clown-gone-wrong dream, of them lying on a blanket sharing a preconcert picnic and a bottle of champagne…

"At least let me pay you for them."

"Oh, for—" He stared at her, clearly exasperated. "You are a hard woman to do something nice for, you know that?"

Wesley had said the same thing. But Wesley was a friend, and Colin was her client. A new one. One she was wildly attracted to and confused by. And guess what, she wasn't going to admit any of that to him. "I'm your PT."

He made a sound of impatience. "I'm aware of that."

"I'm sorry. I'm not…"

Colin strode forward, took her hand and slapped the tickets into her palm. "They're yours. Just forget it and enjoy the concert."

She stood, indecisive, then caught the stubborn set of his features and relented. Refusing again would be rude. "Thank you, Colin."

"You're welcome, geez." He rubbed his lower back. "All that work made my back hurt."

Demi snorted. "Into the massage room. Undressed and on the table. I'll be right in." She closed the door on him, putting the tickets in her pocket. She shouldn't have taken them. But Wesley loved jazz and his birthday was coming up. Maybe he'd like to go with her. Or maybe he'd like to take Cathy. Things seemed to be going well between them.

"Ready."

She went in, almost used to the sight of Colin's incredible physique all laid out for her to touch. Almost. In a few weeks maybe the novelty would wear off to ho-hum. More likely the best she could hope for was to cool her attraction to a manageable level.

Candles lit, music on, hands oiled, she started with the sweeping motions that would improve circulation to his muscles. He was so much looser than when they'd started three weeks before. Unfortunately it was therefore even more of a pleasure to touch him, and stupidly she gave in, keeping her thoughts in platonic territory, but enjoying the smooth masculine feel of his skin, waiting for the muscles to relax further under her fingers. Up to his shoulders, down to his lower back, onto his finely developed gluteals, which the non-PT part of her would call a fabulous ass.

For some reason, instead of loosening, his body stayed tight; his breathing never settled into its usual slow rhythm, the signal she could start going deeper.

A couple of minutes later she broke off, frowning.

"What's up, Colin? You're not relaxing."

"I'm...a little uncomfortable." His voice was low. Not his usual cadence, but not the way he spoke when he was in pain, either.

"How can I help?"

"I could tell you exactly how." This time his tone bordered on suggestive. "But I'm pretty sure you wouldn't like the idea."

Demi's hands stilled. Oh. He was hard. Because *she* was touching him? No, no, he could be enjoying her massage and fantasizing about anyone. Erections happened now and then with her male clients. She knew the protocol. But this was the first time she'd been so flustered.

And so tempted.

She wanted to dig down under his hips and get to know his cock, take it into her mouth until he was begging for mercy, then straddle him on her table, watching his face, listening to his moans, finally having mercy and making him come.

Instead, she took her hands off his back. "Why don't I step out for a few minutes?"

He lifted his head, watching her intently, a question in his eyes. "Is that what you really want to do, Demi?"

Her mouth dropped open in a tiny gasp she couldn't quite suppress. Was he *hitting* on her? No, no, he couldn't be. Wait, maybe he was. "I'll just give you time to get... comfortable again."

"Yeah, okay." His head dropped back to the table, as if

nothing had passed between them. Had she imagined what he was offering?

For three of the longest seconds of her life she stood there, on fire for this man, craving him, wanting to chuck every professional ethic she'd ever had for one fabulous roll on the massage table.

Then she turned quietly, left the room and fled to her office, behind her solid, respectable desk, breath coming fast, cheeks hot—*everything* hot.

Colin Russo had hit on her, and she couldn't do anything about it. In three minutes she was going to have to go back in there and pretend nothing had happened. In three minutes and at all their future appointments.

How could she stand this?

She had to. It was that simple. She hadn't had the world's most tragic life, but it hadn't been a piece of cake, either. She'd been virtually ignored by her parents. The miracle baby they'd prayed for for so long had chosen a damned awkward time to show up, right after they'd adopted two other beautiful children who'd taken to the family culture like ducks to water. While Demi had twisted and chafed and rebelled and sulked and finally put physical and emotional distance between herself and her past in order to let it rest.

If she could do that, she could go into the room with Colin for the last ten minutes of their appointment and not act like a cat in heat. Right?

Right.

Shoulders straight, chest lifted, she marched back into the room, hoping her still-red cheeks were the only thing that would give away her advanced state of fluster. He was sitting up, his naked back broad and muscled.

"Okay now?" She spoke like a nurse asking after her patient's bowel health.

"Fine." He didn't turn around. His voice was flat, withdrawn. Perfect. That was the way she could handle him best.

"Would you like to continue the massage or—"

"I'm good."

"Okay." She stayed by the door. "Don't be surprised if you're sore again tomorrow after today's bike ride. Take it easy for a few days, just gentle walking, and then you can try riding again."

Silence.

"You can get dressed now, and—"

"Demi." His voice had turned gentle.

She kept hers brisk. "Yes?"

"Sorry."

"No problem." She breezed around him to put the cap back on her peppermint oil. "It happens. Nothing to be ashamed of."

"I'm not ashamed of that."

"Oh." She nodded too many times. "Okay. Well, good. I wouldn't want you to—"

"I was apologizing for coming on to you."

"No. You didn't. Not really."

"Yes, I did."

"Oh. Well." She scrubbed at a tiny drop of spilled oil on her counter as if it were a lake of toxic waste. "I didn't notice, so you don't need to—"

"Yes, you did." He reached and clamped a hand down on her wrist, stopping her frenetic scrubbing before she could process that he'd moved. "I saw it in your face."

She had no choice, couldn't hide herself in useless activity anymore. She gave in and met those deep brown eyes, then wished she hadn't when she could barely get her voice to work. "Saw what in my face?"

A slow, sexy grin spread over his features, making it hard for her to breathe, impossible to move.

"How much you wanted it to happen, too."

DEMI PAUSED OUTSIDE her apartment. She was just back from buying fresh ravioli and sauce for dinner. From the end of the hall in the Come to Your Senses communal apartment came voices and laughter.

She fit her key into the lock and turned it. Paused again. Maybe she should go join them for a while? She never did, always felt like an intruder. But in a frustrating catch-22, she would never be one of them unless she spent time feeling like an intruder first.

Not tonight. Socializing took effort; she was tired. Her cozy chair with knitting and audiobook was calling her name. That, with a nice cup of tea or glass of wine after dinner would hit the spot.

A rumble of male voices, then Angela, shrieking with laughter. Demi pushed into her front entranceway, then put the food away in the kitchen and got herself a beer. Took off the top and stood next to her sink. Had the first cold, bubbly sip.

Another rumble of laughter down the hall. She must not have closed her door. She always closed the front door, immediately. She took a few steps toward it, shoving her hand into her back pocket and encountering stiff paper.

The tickets.

She pulled them out, smoothed them on her counter. Saturday. Five days away. Had Colin been trying to soften her up so he could hit on her? She frowned. It hadn't felt like that. More like he thought she had a boring, pathetic life that desperately needed spicing up.

That better not be the reason he hit on her. Geez, at least she only gave him a pity *lunch*.

A clamor of voices sounded from the end of the hall, as if her building-mates were all trying to speak at once.

She looked around her place: sparsely furnished, semi-neat. The big bouquet of flowers from Bonnie Blooms she insisted on treating herself to graced her coffee table. Book-case, a couple of her sister's more tasteful cast-off chairs around a dining table she'd bought herself.

A nice apartment. For a single woman. Who, yes, prob-ably spent too much time at home. One who'd left her door open to the social noise down the hall. She didn't need her psych degree to figure that out.

Clutching her beer, she marched out into the hallway and headed toward the group's common room before she had time to think and change her mind.

At the doorway, she paused, dreading the moment when they noticed her and conversation stopped, then turned po-lite. Maybe she should—

"Hey, Demi's here. She'll know." Jack beckoned her into the room and pointed to the green couch next to Seth. Bon-nie was conspicuously absent—a guilty relief. "Come on, we need the benefit of your wisdom. We're fighting."

"Okay." She plunked onto the couch next to Seth and clinked her bottle with him when he offered. "What do you need to know?"

"We're *not* fighting, we're *discussing.*" Angela glared at Jack. "Why do you think women are more into wed-dings than men?"

"Because men aren't women?" Seth said.

"Because men were out hunting the mammoths and women were stuck in caves." Jack shrugged mischievously. "They had to do something to pass the time, so they de-cided to make the caves pretty."

"What does that have to do with weddings?" Seth asked.

"I think what he means is that the need to make occasions or spaces special and homey evolved as a female trait," Angela said. "Out of utter boredom and total neglect."

"If I may…" Demi pretended to be thinking it over carefully.

"Sure, go ahead, Demi." Jack smiled kindly. "We asked for your opinion and then didn't let you say anything."

"Well, I believe it's more that a woman is really celebrating the joyous day when she finally has cemented in her grip a man whose life she can now proceed to ruin." She waited three beats, then grinned devilishly.

Jack and Seth burst out laughing. Angela, too, though it took her a second.

"While men on the other hand…"

Seth subsided. "Uh-oh."

"…are not taking any of it seriously because they plan to go out and screw the first hot babe they can find no matter what vows they took."

Angela looked stricken. "Demi, do you really believe either of those things?"

"Nah." She grinned, fingering the label on her beer. "I think like any stereotype there is a grain of truth, but it's not true for everyone. According to my mom, Dad was really into all the planning stages of their wedding. Of course he was a control freak. Why were you talking about weddings? Anything I should know?"

Angela blushed. "Saturday night Daniel asked me to marry him."

"Oh, gosh." Without thinking, Demi jumped up and threw herself on Angela in a hug, probably squashing her. "How wonderful. I'm so happy for you."

"Thank you." Angela squeezed her back, laughing with pleasure. "I guess you're not cynical about marriage after all."

"Definitely not. I think it's great. Daniel seems like a

great guy." She wished suddenly that she'd hung around here more, gotten to know him better. So she could say he *was* a great guy, not just that he seemed like one.

"Hey, Demi. How come you never hug *me* like that?" Seth winked at her, which, considering he was one of the best-looking men she'd ever seen, made her want to pull her turtle head back into her shell to avoid answering. Except then he grinned his boy-next-door grin and put her back at ease.

"Hmm. Maybe I will one day."

"All right!" He challenged her with a stare. "When?"

"How about when *you're* getting married?"

"Oh, geez, who am I going to marry? Or more to the point, who'd marry me?"

She sent him the same challenge back. "I'm thinking Bonnie."

For a second she thought she'd gone too far, then a roar erupted from Jack and Angela. Seth, Mr. Cool, Mr. Style, Mr. Mega-Bucks, blushed as if he was fourteen, and thank goodness someone besides her was doing it.

"I gotta hand it to you, Demi." Jack was still chuckling. "None of us have ever had the balls to say it. Hey, Seth, why don't you quit messing around and ask Bonnie to marry you?"

"Seth, I just had a *great* idea." Angela clapped her hands together. "Why don't you quit messing around and ask Bonnie to marry you?"

"Ooh, ooh!" Demi raised her hand as if she were in a classroom. "I had an idea, too. Seth, why don't you quit mess—"

"Stop." Seth looked as if he'd been out in the midday sun for six hours—but he was laughing. "Enough. I'll give it some thought."

The laughter stopped. Angela put a hand to her chest. "You will?"

"There. I just did." He got up and headed for the refrigerator. "I need another beer."

"Get me one, too?" Angela asked.

"Sure. Jack? Demi?"

Demi drained the one she'd brought and nodded, smiling her thanks to Seth, sending silent ones to Colin, who had no idea what he'd started when he handed her those tickets. She was having a good time. And she should also send thanks to Bonnie for not being here so Demi could gain confidence with her other three building-mates before she took on the dragon lady.

"Thanks, Seth." Angela took the beer he handed her. "Here's to your wedding."

"Hear, hear!" Jack raised his.

"Oh, I'm thinking a triple wedding now." Angela set her sights on Jack. "When are you going to ask Melissa?"

"There's the real question," Seth said.

"Ha!" Jack scowled. "When are you going to mind your own business?"

"And, Demi." Angela gestured with her bottle. "How about whatsisname, Colin?"

"You're seeing someone?" Seth seemed surprised.

"No." She shook her head adamantly. "He's a client. Angela has fallen deeply in love with him because he's hot."

"Wow." Seth settled back onto the couch next to her. "That is so deep."

"*I* just look," Angela protested. "*She* gets to touch him. *Everywhere.*"

"Not *everywhere.*" Demi was having a hard time keeping a straight face. For some reason, instead of the situation with Colin being an anguished source of conflict, in this company it was simply funny.

"What do you do when you're attracted to a client?" Jack asked. "Can you ask him out?"

"No, no, no." She waggled her finger. "Big bad idea. Prosecutable in fact."

"Now, wait a minute," Angela said. "Bonnie saw you two strolling down the sidewalk together last week. At lunchtime."

"Oh, call the paper," Jack said. "Post on Facebook. Tweet the world. They were on the sidewalk."

"Oh, that. No, that was nothing. We'd finished a session—"

"With *massage?*" Angela asked.

"Yes." Demi stopped the oncoming rush of comments with a raised hand. "I end most sessions with massage."

"I can see it now." Seth framed his hands around a headline. "'Client in critical pleasure condition after massage veers out of control.'"

Demi pretended to ignore him. "We were both hungry and—"

"After a solid hour." Seth had switched to a booming newscaster's voice. "We were still starved for each other."

"—so we ate a couple of hot dogs in the park."

"Authorities believe dogs were involved."

"Eww, *Seth*." Angela made a face. "That is disgusting."

"I know, I know." He switched to his normal voice. "But it was either that or an eat-my-wiener joke."

"Disgusting too-o!" Angela sang.

"As I was saying." Demi continued to ignore him. "At the park we *ingested frankfurters,* and then he went home."

"Client retreats." Jack took up the newscast. "'She was too much for me,' he admits."

Demi collapsed into giggles with the others, loving the glow of being part of the gang, at least this one time.

"So besides all the perverted male commentary, the

point is, Colin wanted to have lunch with you." Angela was beaming encouragingly. "That's great. Now, if he calls just to talk, you know he wants more."

"He isn't going to call me just to talk. I'm totally not his—"

Her phone rang. A roar erupted in the room. Demi's adrenaline went nuts. She grabbed the phone and stared. Her sister. "It's *not* him."

"Doesn't matter. You should have seen your face." Angela was grinning at her. "Like you wanted to run and hide, and jump up and down with joy at the same time."

"Oh, come on."

"I'm right. And when was the last time all of us felt that way when a certain someone might be calling?"

Jack raised his hand impatiently.

"Let's see…why don't we hear from…Jack." Angela gave him royal permission.

"When I was falling in love with Melissa."

"Correct." Angela pointed to herself. "When I was falling in love with Daniel."

Seth put a hand to his heart. "Last night when I heard my take-out pizza was ready."

"Guys…" Demi gestured helplessly in the face of a triple set of knowing grins.

"It's unanimous. I'm right." Angela pointed a warning finger at Demi. "Trust me here, girlfriend. You are about to enter a brave new world o' man-trouble."

6

BONNIE STOOD FACING Don on the front steps of Come to Your Senses, thinking a good-night kiss was a really good idea. Dinner had been delicious, sushi at Umi Sake House, where they'd had sake until she lost track of how much. Right now she was feeling no pain, the air was bracingly chilly and Don was looking particularly handsome in the building's outdoor light. He was a good-looking guy, a few inches taller than Bonnie, with a solid broad-shouldered build, dirty-blond hair he kept neatly combed and big brown eyes with long lashes. Kind of a Ricky Gervais face, very cute. For their date he'd worn a navy sport coat over dress khakis. She liked that he'd gone traditional. She'd worn a new dress—new to her anyway—one of those miracle secondhand-store finds that fit perfectly and cost nearly nothing. It wasn't her usual wildly patterned Bohemian type outfit, but a light blue knit that clung in very flattering ways.

She was gratified to notice Don had discreetly checked out her bod whenever she stood or leaned over. Dating a gentleman was great, and a wonderful change from Seth the Sexual Barbarian, but Bonnie wanted a guy with a nice, healthy libido, too, and apparently Don had one.

"Don, I had a great time tonight."

"I did, too." He grinned at her. "I always have a great time with you, Bonnie."

"Same here." She smiled back expectantly, willing him to make the big move. She was perfectly able to initiate the kiss, but she was particular about two things in the dating world: that the first kiss and the marriage proposal were the man's jobs.

"Would you like to go out in a couple of days? Maybe Wednesday?"

"I'd love that." She moved a step closer, put her hand on his lapel, looked up invitingly. *Kiss me, you fool.*

"Maybe we could go sailing if it's not too cold?"

"Oh, I'd love that." She blinked. Sailing? On what?

"I have a sailboat. Nothing fancy, but I'd love you to meet her."

She was so thrilled he owned a boat—a boat!—that she ignored him referring to "meeting her" as if it were human.

"I'm not fancy, either, so that works perfectly." She smoothed her hand over his shirtfront. Nice firm chest underneath. Very nice. *Now, Don, about that kiss...*

"You're great, Bonnie. Really great."

"So are you..." She rose on tiptoe toward his face. Apparently she'd have to get this one going by herself.

However.

Once she turned the green-light signal into a roaring bonfire of come-on-already, Don took over.

Oh, boy, did he.

His arms came around her in the kind of hug that let a woman know she was really being held. His mouth found hers perfectly on the first try, and their kiss was soft and lingering, no slobber whatsoever, with promise of good heat to come.

Mmm, yes. Maybe she'd fall for him one day. She really, really hoped so.

The kiss ended slowly, and then there was another one, and another after that, and Bonnie was starting to heat up quite nicely and about to press herself shamelessly against his khakis to let him know, when the door to the building opened behind them.

"What the—"

An angry male voice. Very angry. *Seth*.

Bonnie's instinct was to jump guiltily away, but she managed to squash it in time. Not hard, since Don's arms were still solidly around her and she would have had to shove him to get anywhere.

"What's going on, Bonnie?"

Don turned, keeping Bonnie partly behind him. "Is there a problem?"

Seth stepped forward, gray eyes blazing, nearly a head taller than Don. He was wearing a black leather jacket and gray shirt. Behind him the door swung shut with a melodramatic clank.

"Seth, chill out." Bonnie spoke quickly, putting a reassuring hand on Don's shoulder. "Don, this is Seth, a friend of mine who is being a little overprotective at the moment. Seth, this is Don. My *date*."

She sent Seth a back-off look that had better work, because if he tried to mess this up, she was never speaking to him again.

"Nice to meet you." Don managed to make the pleasantry sound like an insult.

Seth nodded once, lips tight. "Nice to meet you, too."

An even worse insult. Bonnie sighed. Men and their egos.

"Bonnie, you okay?"

"More than, Seth."

"Good." He pushed past them, ran down the steps and stalked off down Olive. Bonnie and Don both turned to watch him go.

"That was weird," Don said.

"Tell me about it."

"You got any more of those *protective* guys hanging around?"

"Nope. Oh." She grimaced. "Well, there's Jack…"

Don looked pained. "Jack, huh."

"He's a sweetheart. And semiengaged."

Don sighed. "I guess it doesn't surprise me. I'd go nuts if I walked in on some guy kissing you, too."

Bonnie bussed his cheek gratefully. He'd dealt with Seth's little tantrum really well. Point in his favor. Maybe he trusted her instinctively. Maybe he just hadn't been bitten by the dark side of love yet, making him suspicious and bitter. Though she couldn't imagine any person single and on the downward slope toward thirty who didn't have scars of some kind.

"I don't think you need to worry." She turned toward him again, heart still thumping from the encounter with Seth, trying to block the image of his tall body all in black, striding away from her.

"No?" Don gathered her close. "No special guy in your life?"

"None." The phrase hurt just a little, but it was true.

Don kissed her again, this time harder, more possessively, and she tried to throw herself into it, tried to banish memories of other lips, and succeeded nicely. Pretty nicely. Sort of nicely. *Oh, Seth.* "I'd like to keep it that way, Bonnie. If you're willing."

She'd already forgotten what they were talking about. "I'm sorry, keep who what way?"

He chuckled. "I know. After that kiss I can't think straight, either."

"No, I know." Oh, dear. That wasn't what had distracted her.

She suddenly wanted the evening over, wanted to go back to her apartment and regroup, process more of this damn endless grief at finally giving up on Seth so she could concentrate on falling for Don. He was really a great guy, generous and funny and sweet.

"I was asking if we could date exclusively, Bonnie. I think I'm fall— I'm crazy about you."

"Oh." She breathed the syllable out, wishing he could have made the declaration about ten minutes earlier, when the evening was still all about him. "Same here. And yes. I'd like that. Definitely. Yes."

"Good." He squeezed her tightly, kissed her with real passion this time, and enough desire that her brain came back completely into the date so she could respond more genuinely. "I'm really happy, Bonnie."

"Me, too." She wanted, suddenly and absurdly, to cry. "Really happy."

"So I'll see you Wednesday, then?"

"Yes. Wednesday."

His eyes were warm, kind, and he gave her a sweet, long kiss before he whispered good-night.

He hadn't hit on her. He hadn't asked himself in for coffee. He'd kissed her, asked permission to date her exclusively and had gone home.

Wow. A nice guy. A really, really nice one. Finally.

She watched him walk away, thinking how great it was to see a guy's back and not feel agony, to trust she'd see him again, and that things between them would go forward until they reached an impasse or they grew old and died.

Normal. Date a guy like him, see if things worked out.

None of the glitches and fears and games and exhausting heart-and-mind gymnastics. For once she felt safe and relaxed going into a relationship.

Imagine that.

Upstairs, Bonnie opened the door to her apartment and was greeted by the basket of laundry she'd intended to get up early and do that morning, then intended to do on her lunch hour, then intended to do before her date...

Oops.

Sighing, she took off her jacket and flung it onto a nearby chair, then frowned down at the basket. Since she was washing anyway, she might as well add the dress.

She wriggled out of it and added it to the pile, then kicked off her shoes and tossed in her stockings and underwear. She'd shower, put on pj's, then do laundry.

Her phone rang from her jacket and she grabbed for it. Seth? No. Geez, Bonnie.

"Hi, Don." She smiled, wondering what he'd do if he could see what she wasn't wearing. "You home yet?"

"Almost. I missed hearing your voice."

"Aww." She grinned and ran her hand over her breasts, imagining him touching them. What would that touch be like? Would he be able to bring her nearly to orgasm with his fingers and mouth on them? "I'm glad you called. I was thinking about you."

"Good thoughts?"

"All good."

"I'm glad. So...listen, that guy who interrupted us."

"Seth?" She tensed, palm still curved around her right breast.

"You used to date him, didn't you."

Bonnie closed her eyes. His tone was calm, but she didn't know him well enough to sense what he was feeling. "About five years ago."

"It's not over for him."

She didn't know what to say. "I don't think—"

"It wasn't a question. I'm telling you, it's not over for him."

"Oh. Well. I suppose—"

"Before I get in any deeper, Bonnie, I need to know if it's over for you." He coughed, cleared his throat, coughed again.

"It's over." She spoke clearly, feeling only slightly sick. It wasn't a lie. She was well on her way to being over Seth, and the more she was with Don, the more distant their connection would seem.

"That makes me really happy."

She smiled; her hand moved over her breasts again. "I'm glad."

"I'm really looking forward to seeing what we can be together."

"Same here." She imagined herself taking off his sport coat, tossing it across the room. Unbuttoning his shirt—would he have hair on his chest or not? "I have to wait for Wednesday to see you again?"

"How about now?" He laughed softly. "Okay, maybe that would be pushing it."

She giggled like a silly schoolgirl, hand drifting down over her stomach. "I'm free tomorrow…"

"I can't." He made a growling sound of frustration. "I have a work dinner. I guess we have to keep it Wednesday."

"I guess." She sighed heavily.

"Bonnie."

"Mmm?"

"I can't wait to get my arms around you again."

"Me neither." Her hand found its way lower. "Maybe we should have dinner at my place?"

Argh! What had she said? She couldn't afford to make

any kind of decent dinner for him with her finances in a crisis state. Cottage cheese with a side of potato chips. Maybe without the potato chips.

"Actually, I was going to suggest I make dinner for you here."

Whew. "I'd love that, thank you." She smiled dreamily. Dinner at his no-doubt fancy apartment, nice wine, then a trip into his no-doubt very masculine bedroom. What kind of lover would he be? Sensitive and sweet, maybe a hidden beast in there somewhere...

Her hand brushed idly across her breasts, back down. "Can I bring wine?"

"I'll have plenty. Come early. We should make a night of it." His voice was low, suggestive.

"Mmm, I'd really like that." She echoed his tone, fingers lingering between her legs.

"Good night then, Bonnie. Sweet dreams. I'll call you tomorrow."

"Good night, Don." She hung up, smiling, and let herself slump against the wall. Dinner, wine, romance. Who could ask for anything more?

She imagined herself under him, his body thrusting hard. Her fingers went to work; she let her head drop back, braced herself, arching her back. What did Don sound like when he came? What did he look like? She wanted to see. She wanted to see him coming, feel him inside her. She wanted him to—

Her door swung open. "Bonnie?"

She gasped. Seth.

Oh, dear God.

For a long moment their eyes held, his gray ones glittering in a face stony with shock. The only sound was Bonnie's loud, irregular breathing.

Seeing him when she was prepared was bad enough.

Seeing him when she was naked and horny and touching herself…

Please, God, give her strength to resist the inevitable. Seth wouldn't let an opportunity like this go by to press his advantage, fight his case, try to get her back with sex, the crazy, irresistibly explosive way they went about it.

Oh, Seth.

His gaze traveled down her body. His eyes closed. His jaw and fist clenched.

"Sorry. I should have knocked."

Then he turned and walked away.

"SO THEN MIKE hits a patch of gravel and wipes out." Nick smacked his fist into his palm. He and Colin were walking the three-mile Elliott Bay Trail from Smith Cove Park north then back south, along the railroad and the Sound into downtown Seattle. They had nearly completed the trail and were about to turn and head back. "I'm telling you, everyone there was thinking about you when he fell, but he turned out fine."

"That's good." Colin swung along, his body itching to run. He'd been feeling better every day, looser, in less pain, and had decided to try a walk. At the last minute, he'd called Nick to join him, well aware that asking Nick to take a walk was like asking a master engineer to change a lightbulb. Colin thought he'd be glad for the company but Nick had done nothing but talk training: running, biking and swimming. He might as well have applied thumbscrews, though Colin had the uncomfortable impression that those topics might have been all they ever talked about. Now the story of Mike, who'd fallen a hell of a lot harder than Colin, and was completely fine. Of course.

They turned at the Sculpture Garden and started on the three miles back to Colin's car and Nick's bike.

"I did a personal best in the pool the other day. I was smoking, man. It was like—"

"Want to run?" Colin broke into a slow, careful jog, not waiting for Nick to respond. He couldn't stand it anymore.

"Are you kidding?" Nick's freckled face broke into a grin. "Hell, yeah. That baby pace was killing me."

Baby. Thanks, Nick. Colin accelerated, monitoring his back for signs of rebellion. So far so good. And God did it feel good to move, even running like a beginner. The air blew fresher, the colors around them seemed brighter, the Sound glistened restlessly in the sunlight. Another unusually warm day for late October. The gods were smiling today.

"How's that feeling?" Nick turned to scope out Colin's stride, his sandy curls blowing haphazardly in the breeze.

"Good. Really good."

"Think you can go faster?"

"Sure." He wasn't sure. But why not try? If he felt any pain, he'd slow or stop immediately. Otherwise Demi would have his head on a platter. He grinned at the thought, then forced himself to concentrate on his body and his stride. Demi occupied way too many of his thoughts recently. "You talked to Stephanie lately?"

"Oh. Yeah. I, uh, saw her last night."

"Yeah?" He felt a twinge of jealousy, even knowing it was entirely innocent and bound to happen. Nick and Stephanie ran in the same social circles. Of course they'd bump into each other. "How did she look?"

"Fantastic."

Colin gave him a sharp glance. Nick's response had been a little too enthusiastic for his taste. "Yeah? She seem happy?"

"She does actually." Nick measured his pace to match Colin's. "Really happy."

Colin sped up. He wanted Stephanie to be happy. At the same time, news of her looking miserable without him wouldn't have hurt. "Maybe I'll call her. See how she's doing."

"Yeah. Yeah, sure." Nick's enthusiasm had fallen off.

"Maybe she'd like to have lunch with me."

"Maybe."

Colin inhaled deeply. His muscles were warm, his back was quiet, accepting that this was what it was meant to do. He ran faster and the extra speed fed his energy. Check this out! The King of the Track was on his way back. Not going to compete again? Said who? Look at him! That finish line in Hawaii would be facing him yet. "Damn, this feels great."

"You look good, man. Keep it up."

They kept the pace going, joining the railroad tracks at Garfield and following them until they'd head back south again to Smith's Cove. Demi would be proud of him. Well, no, she'd probably yell at him for taking the chance, but look how it was working—

He stumbled and pitched forward. A stab of pain shot through his back, but he caught himself before he fell. He stopped running immediately to assess the damage.

Nick jogged back to him. "Geez, buddy, you okay?"

"Yeah." He tried to hide the fact that he was breathing a hell of a lot harder than Nick, and twisted experimentally, tried out a few stretches, then grinned. No pain whatsoever. "I'm fine."

"Thank God." Nick slapped him on the back, grinning. "Nothing keeps you down, huh?"

"Nothing." Colin held up his hand for a high five and they kept running, egging each other on to faster speeds until Colin's navy Toyota came into sight next to Nick's bike. Nick sprinted on ahead, as Colin knew he would.

Once a competitor, always a competitor. Though at least Colin had the sense not to join that race.

Nick started laughing when Colin reached his car. "Listen to you, panting like a girl."

"You wait. I'll live to kick your ass at the world championship." He forced his breathing to slow, unlocked the car and grabbed his water bottle. "Want to go for a beer?"

"You kidding? I have many more miles to go before I drink. This was my warm-up, old man."

"Right. Seeya." He waved Nick off, envious that he got to keep going, but determined not to be stupid about this. He'd promised Demi that much, and he owed it to himself, as well. So far everything felt good. Everything. He wanted to run the same trail again right now, then plow into the water and swim to Alaska. He wanted to sit down and indulge his visualization of winning Hawaii.

Instead, he walked until his muscles had cooled, did his core exercises and a series of long, careful stretches before he climbed back into his car and drove home, windows open, radio blasting a Red Hot Chili Peppers CD. He even got looks from a few women crossing the street, something that hadn't happened in a while.

Colin was on his way back!

At home, he took ibuprofen and showered, made himself a late-afternoon turkey sandwich on whole-grain bread bought from Angela's bakery and drank a good quart of water to make sure he stayed hydrated. Then he treated himself to a beer and the newspaper. And another beer. What a great evening. He felt as if he could breathe more deeply; his body felt alive and glowing. God, he'd missed working out. Look what it did for him. He even felt enough like his old self to consider calling Stephanie tonight, see how she was, find out if she was really that happy or if she missed him, if she wanted to get together and talk things over.

After his second beer, he opened a third and picked up the phone, feeling more nervous than he should be. He'd known this woman forever. A lot had changed with his accident, but not that.

"Hey, Stephanie."

"…Colin." She sounded surprised, but not necessarily in a good way. She hadn't expected his call, and undoubtedly hearing his voice brought back a lot of emotion. "I'm out shopping. With Briana. What's up? Why are you calling me?"

"To see how you are." She'd sounded slightly irritated, which irritated him. After all they'd meant to each other, she was cranky he'd interrupted her shopping?

"Oh. Well, I'm fine. Doing really well. Happy."

He hadn't expected that. "Don't miss me, huh."

"We broke up for a reason, Colin." She sounded as if she was lecturing a small whiny boy, even though he'd deliberately kept his voice playful and flirtatious. He'd forgotten how much that tone pissed him off.

"I know." He took a deep breath. "I was an ass, Stephanie. I'm sorry. But things are finally turning around."

"That's great, Colin. I'm glad for you." She didn't sound glad. She sounded like all she cared about was getting back to spending money.

"Yeah, thanks." He was totally disoriented. He'd called to ask her out, start the process of getting back together with her, and now that he had her on the phone, this woman he'd adored and wanted to marry, he felt oddly detached. Wasn't even sure he cared about seeing her again. Wasn't even sure she was the same woman. And yet, of course she was.

Maybe he wasn't the same man.

"Was that all?"

"I was wondering if you wanted to go out sometime. To

catch up." The second the words were out, he wanted them back. This didn't feel right.

"Colin…"

She wasn't going to give him a chance, and faced with that fact, he was stunned to find he didn't really care, not deep down where it mattered. "What, Stephanie?"

"I'm seeing someone else."

"Okay." The word came out automatically. Along with it, a loosening of the tension that had been holding him. "Who? Do I know him?"

"Look, this isn't really the time to have this discussion."

Wariness rose. "Giving me a name is a discussion?"

"You always turn everything into a fight."

"I'm not fight—"

"That looks great on you, Briana. Colin, I have to go. I'll call you later."

No, she wouldn't. He was about to tell her that when the pieces clicked into place. How stupid could he be? "Nick."

Silence.

Oh, for—

"You're seeing *Nick*."

"It just happened, Colin. I'm sorry. Neither of us planned this."

"And neither of you thought it was worth telling me."

"Of course. But— I mean, of course we— It just never seemed—"

"Yeah. Okay, never mind. Keep shopping. Buy out the store." He hung up the phone, already regretting the bitter comment. He should have taken the high road, wished her well, wished her happiness screwing one of his best friends when they'd only broken up a few weeks ago. Or no, months. But after four years of dating—

Nice.

Back when he'd been whole and stepped in bad crap like

this, he'd jump on his bike, take a punishing ride around Seattle's steepest streets, come back utterly spent, then sleep and wake up refreshed and revived. Worked like magic.

But he wasn't whole now. One puny walk/run had used up his allotment of exercise for the day. He couldn't do anything to help himself.

A completely inappropriate urge to call Demi came over him. Geez, he needed a mommy to cry to now?

He'd deal with this like a real man. Get a six-pack, turn on the TV and get blitzed.

Two hours later, the six-pack was gone and he felt like absolute hell. Men were really stupid when it came to handling emotion.

He got up, his body slightly stiff, swallowed more ibuprofen, took off his clothes and crawled into bed though it was barely eight o'clock.

In his dream, Stephanie was stripping for him, tossing the clothes onto his face, then laughing at him because he couldn't have her. He tried to lunge for her, tried to show her who was in charge here, but his body wouldn't move. He couldn't get out of bed.

Then disembodied hands helped lift him. Hands that knew exactly what they were doing, soothing his aches, giving back his power. Stephanie's image grew fuzzy; her hair started turning dark. A dimple dented her chin. The hands on him belonged to Demi now, stroking his chest, flicking over his nipples. Then she was on top of him, her hair dragging across his skin, her mouth reaching his cock, which strained toward her, desperate for the feel of her tongue.

Then he was inside her mouth, so hot and hard that he came almost instantly, in a glorious, pulsing release.

And woke to horrible pain ripping through his back.

7

"Ahhh." Demi relaxed in her chair and pulled her knitting onto her lap. Today had been good. She'd released one client into the world, his frozen shoulder healed to the point where he could manage his recovery on his own now. She loved that, when she'd really been able to make a difference in someone's life. Her client had been so grateful, he'd brought in a bouquet of flowers, which were sitting right now on Demi's dining table. White roses and mini-carnations, blue delphinium and hydrangea. Just gorgeous.

After work, Demi had taken advantage of the dry, warm Tuesday and gone for a long run, then back to Come to Your Senses for a shower and to change into loose, comfortable clothes, followed by a dinner of pasta with mushrooms and greens and a glass of wine. Then another glass. A third sat on the table next to her beside a ripe pear and shortbread cookies. She inserted the earbuds of her headphones and pressed Play to listen to her book. Perfect. A night of quiet relaxing. Just what she—

Her phone rang. Of course.

Demi put her knitting aside—was she *ever* going to have time to finish the sweater?—struggled out of the seductive depths of her chair and ran for her phone, which she'd carelessly left on the kitchen counter. When she planned to indulge in an evening of total relaxation, having the phone within easy reach was vital.

It was Colin. She calmed herself, made sure she was still breathing normally, and answered. "Hey, Colin."

"Demi." His voice was tight.

Uh-oh. "What's wrong?"

"Can't move."

"You can't move?" Demi frowned, glancing longingly at her chair. "Want to tell me what you were doing that brought this on?"

"Sleeping."

"Sleeping. That's it?" Silence. Demi sighed. "That's not it. Out with it."

"I went running. Slowly. I was fine after that. Then I took a nap and…uh, when I woke up I couldn't move."

Demi thought that one over. Either he hadn't been running slowly, or something had happened between the nap and waking up that had trashed his back. She didn't want to know what. Especially if it involved a hot woman riding him like a pony.

Grrr. She'd told him he had to be careful. "How long have you been awake?"

"A couple of hours. I thought it would loosen up."

"No." She sighed. "You need to relieve the spasms. Can you call your doctor or get to a pharmacy? Muscle relaxers should help some."

"I can't get out of bed." Spoken as if she should have figured that out herself.

Demi narrowed her eyes. "So what are you calling me for?"

"I'll pay you double, triple, whatever you want, if you come help me."

"Oh, for God's sake. You go out and do something stupid and you expect me to come fix it at ten o'clock at night?"

"I don't *expect* anything. I'm asking. If you can't come, forget it. I'll just lie here until the stench of my corpse brings in the neighbors."

An unwilling chuckle escaped her. He hadn't lost his sense of humor this time. "I don't make house calls."

"Think of it as a mobile-treatment unit."

Demi sighed, wistfully contemplating her wine, her cookies, her chair, her book…

But then there was Colin.

Oh, man. She had to be completely insane even thinking of going over there at this hour. To his house. To his *bedroom*. When last time they'd been together he'd all but asked her to sleep with him.

Completely insane.

Outright bonkers.

Nutty in the extreme.

"Give me your address." She headed for the pad by her kitchen counter and wrote down the address of his building, along with the name of the neighbor who would buzz her in. "Okay. I'll be there in fifteen."

She ended the call and kicked off her ugly fuzzy slippers, the most comfortable footwear on earth, thought about changing out of her sweats to look more attractive, then very sensibly decided against it. After picking up a few supplies, she slipped out her apartment door.

All the way to Colin's house, Demi grumbled to herself. Why was she helping him? He'd fall back asleep eventually. His spasms would work themselves out. She didn't need to be doing this.

So why was she?

Ahem. She should avoid answering that question honestly. Because it had to do with concepts like titillation, temptation and tantalization.

Masochist. She should know better. Except in Colin's case, apparently she didn't. Or just didn't care.

She pulled up to his building, an attractive one on Eighth Avenue in the University District. Having parked in a visitor spot, she went inside and rang his neighbor's buzzer. Seconds later, the front door clicked open and she went inside, took the elevator to the third floor and emerged onto a well-lit hallway with gray carpet and cream-colored doors. She read the gold numbers as she padded by, stopping opposite Thirty-two to retrieve his spare key, which his neighbor had shoved so it just showed under the door.

Okay. Moment of truth. His place: Thirty-four. She let herself in, in full professional mode, keeping nerves at bay by holding on to her irritation that Colin hadn't taken care of himself. Whether it was the run or sex with someone or whatever he'd been doing in bed—she did not want to know—he'd been careless to backslide like this when he was doing so well.

"Hello?" The condo was modern, spare, with a fireplace in the living room and a fabulous view of the city from floor-to-ceiling windows. She put the key on the kitchen counter and crossed the space toward the door that must be his bedroom. Dark.

Oh, boy. She couldn't believe she was doing this. Into the lion's den…

"Colin?"

"Yeah, here. Light's right there next to you."

She flipped it on and walked over the condo-predictable soft beige carpet to the queen bed in the middle of the room, thinking how much more she liked the hardwood floors, worn fixtures and unexpected spaces in her apartment.

"So." She stood by his bed, hands on her hips, feeling suddenly shaky-nervous. "You've done it, huh."

"I guess." His face was pale and drawn, eyes shadowed with pain.

Her heart ached. Yes, he'd been a dummy, but what a tough setback. "Do you have naproxen sodium?"

"No."

"I brought some." She brought the bottle out of her purse. "Two every twelve hours. Starting now."

"Yes, Nurse Anderson."

"I'll get you water." She marched into the kitchen, noticing more this time: his sax on the couch, a neat pile of running magazines on the glass coffee table, modern art prints on the walls—not exactly her taste, but colorful, and a nice antidote to the bland interior. On a table outside the kitchen, a rack of exquisite knives, blades gracefully shaped in assorted sizes, handles of various materials: wood, metal and…bone? Really lovely. How long since he'd made the last one? An unusual talent.

In the kitchen she opened a cabinet. Four glasses, four plates, four mugs and a lot of empty space. Apparently he wasn't much for entertaining large groups.

She filled a glass with water and brought it back into the bedroom. "Here."

"Thanks." He reached for the glass, grunting with the strain, and took the pills.

"Those will help. Can you turn over?"

"No."

"I'll take care of that first, then we'll work on some pressure massage." Demi turned his light back off so the only illumination was outside light coming through the open curtains and the apartment light coming through his bedroom door.

"Don't have any candles, sorry."

She snorted. "Not a problem."

"You can spray aftershave on the bed if you want. And how about some real music?"

"Yeah, thanks, Colin. I think we'll make do with this setup as is." She kicked off her shoes, pulled off her sweater, attempting her very hardest to look nonchalant, and climbed onto the bed next to him. As she helped to roll him over, she tried not to notice the sleepy-clean smell of his skin, the warmth of his body and the cool softness of the sheets. Or that he was stark naked. She was here in a medical capacity, not to take off her own clothes and slide in next to him.

Oh, what a bad idea. And speaking of bad ideas, she shouldn't have had that extra glass of wine with dinner because it was making her wanton thoughts and impulses a lot harder to ignore. The dim light wasn't helping, either, though she felt it important to make him relax.

Not that she'd get wild sex out of a guy who couldn't move.

"Here." She maneuvered one of the four bed pillows under his hips, then knelt beside him and put her hands on his back, finding it very difficult to feel professional when she was in bed with him.

In fact, she didn't feel professional at all.

And when she started to massage, experiencing his tightness gradually release under her fingers, she found herself becoming more and more sensual in her motions, enjoying the texture of his skin, of his muscles, his back, his extraordinary buttocks, his absolute maleness.

What was she doing? What was she considering? She wanted to slide her hands under his hips to feel if he was hard from her touch.

This was crazy. "Better?"

"Mmmm." His voice was a low growl that made her shivery. "Much."

"Good. Can you turn over now?"

"I can, but you probably wouldn't want me to."

"Oh." She closed her eyes. He was hard again. Oh, my.

"Sorry. But you are very sexy, and…we are in bed together."

"We are." She nearly purred the words. *Shh, careful, Demi.*

He turned his head, features just visible in the half light, and for a moment she imagined herself so vividly leaning over to kiss him that she started swaying forward and had to stop herself.

"Help me turn on my side toward you."

"Yes, sir." She covered him to his waist with the sheet and lifted his left side, arranged a pillow at his back and one between his knees. "Okay?"

"Yes. Now lie down next to me."

"Uh, Colin?" Her breath started coming faster in spite of her attempts to stay calm. "I don't think that's a good idea."

"I can't move. What am I going to do to you?"

"I don't want to find out."

"Yes, you do."

Yes, she did. Desperately. She was crazy with hunger for this man, even if he was immobilized.

"Lie down. I want you next to me. Please."

Oh, crap. When would she stop being victim to her hormones?

Telling herself she'd gone completely over the edge, she closed her eyes, slid down onto the mattress a foot away from him, even more stiff than he'd been when he was rigid with pain.

"Closer."

"Don't push it."

"Closer. Or I'll hurt myself and it will be your fault."

"Hurt yourself doing what?"

"Demi." His voice had dropped to a seductive murmur. "Come closer."

She swallowed audibly. Then slowly, with an exhausting combination of reluctance and eagerness, she wiggled closer to his warm body.

"Good." His hand landed on her solar plexus and lay still, exciting and oddly reassuring. "Thank you."

She swallowed again. "Colin…"

"Shh, relax." His hand began to move over her, slowly and carefully, from the right side of her rib cage to the left. "Just let me touch you like this."

Demi closed her eyes, heart beating much too quickly, breath coming much too fast. Caught in the world's oldest dilemma: what she should do versus what she wanted to do.

She wanted him. She wanted his hands all over her body the way hers had been all over his so many times. Only closer, more intimate. Sexual.

His hand veered from its back-and-forth path, making warm circles up under her breasts, down between her hip bones. She felt herself grow hungry, wet between her legs, the area crying out for his hand to explore, his fingers to bury themselves deeply in her.

She swallowed again. This shouldn't be happening. But in his territory, in his bed, want had triumphed. She felt less like his PT and more like…a woman. A desirable, sexy woman, wanted by a much more desirable, sexy man. Who could get enough of that feeling?

Not really excuses for breaking professional ethics to this degree. But she was nearly past caring, on fire for him to touch her, touch her *there*.

He took his time, finally sliding his hand under her soft, worn T-shirt, up between her breasts. Then he stopped; he drew his breath in sharply.

"Colin." She was instantly concerned. "You shouldn't be moving if—"

"No, no. It's not pain." He resumed stroking her, keeping his fingers together, investigating her sternum.

"What is it, then?" she whispered.

"You're not wearing a bra."

"Oh." She moved restlessly, becoming crazy aroused. "I left the house quickly."

"I like that about you. A lot." He spread his fingers, hand still centered between her breasts, but on this stroke his thumb and pinkie slid over her nipples and she was the one inhaling sharply. "You're beautiful, Demi."

She didn't know what to say to that. She was decidedly not. Attractive on a good day. Not beautiful.

His hand slid full onto her right breast. She let out a moan. "Colin."

"Mmm?"

"This…can't go anywhere."

"I think you'd be surprised."

"I mean, I can't and you can't… Your back."

"I know." His hand slid down her stomach; his fingers slipped under the loose waistband of her sweats, just touched the top of her pelvic bone and slid back up.

She exhaled explosively. This was torture. She should stop him. She should get up and walk out. She should…

"Pull down your sweats."

She swallowed again. Pulled them down. His hand followed the motion, roamed over her panties, the heat of his skin penetrating the thin cotton covering.

Demi groaned. All reason had gone, replaced by the searing need to have his hands directly on her.

"Take your panties off," he whispered.

She obeyed, practically weeping with desire.

"Spread your legs for me."

They opened wide off to his right, avoiding hitting his body.

Then nothing. No movement, no sound but their breathing, the room's air cool on her wet sex, sensitivity heightened by arousal and anticipation.

Then his palm gripped her hip bone, fingertips nearly reaching where she wanted them to be.

Nearly.

"Do you want me to touch you, Demi?"

"Yes."

"Where?"

She took his hand, guided it, let out a moan when his fingers found their target.

"Ohhh." His voice was a deep groan of appreciation. "Feel that."

"Yes."

"You're wet for me."

"Yes." She lifted her hips, panting, squeezing her buttocks together.

He gently explored, stroking her labia, lightly flicking over her clitoris, then leaving to explore again, coming back to her clit more and more frequently until he settled in a firm, circular rhythm.

Demi practically lifted off the bed. She barely had time to register the change before her orgasm started to build, then swept over her.

She gave in to the waves of pleasure, cried out his name, losing herself completely to the ecstasy, on and on, while she panted and writhed, and then slowly, slowly came down.

Oh, my. She hadn't come that hard in a long, long time.

"God, you are hot, Demi." His whisper was harsh, choked. "That was… Oh, my God."

She came back slowly to herself, aware of his lingering hand, aware of his body so close.

"What…what can I do for you?"

He chuckled. "You just did it."

"But don't you—"

"Hey, Ms. PT." He spoke softly beside her. "What would be the worst thing for my back right now?"

"Oh." She laughed, put her hands to her face, then let them fall beside her head. "Right. Tension and spasms."

"Uh-huh. I'll take a rain check."

She turned her head, on level with his. "This was not… I mean, I really can't—"

"Can't do this again. Right. And before you did this you couldn't do this, either."

"I know."

"And before we went to lunch you couldn't go to lunch, and before—"

"I *know,* I know."

"Does this feel like a mistake?" He moved his hand to lie possessively across her stomach.

"It will tomorrow."

"Do me a favor."

"Uh-oh."

"Hey." He gave her an affectionate pinch. "Since I just did the hardest work of my entire life staying still with my back relaxed while every instinct was screaming at me to plunge inside you, I think I'm due a small favor."

She giggled. "What?"

"Spend the night."

Demi arched away from him. "Colin, I cannot spend—"

"You know what, Demi?"

She sighed. "What?"

"If you want to be happier, we need to get you out of that rut of negativity, change it to a positive can-do attitude."

Demi burst out laughing. "Oh, really."

"Repeat after me. 'I can-do some sleeping here tonight.'"

"I can see you're completely insane."

"Very good." He squeezed her abdomen. "Next. 'I can-do lunch sometimes with Colin.'"

"I can see where this is going."

"Excellent. And the most important can-do is this one. 'I can-do Colin whenever he wants me to.'"

She was giggling so hard she snorted, which made her giggle even harder. "You always get what you want?"

"Doesn't everyone?"

"No!"

He was still grinning, and he looked so pleasant and relaxed it was impossible to imagine he'd been unable to move so recently. And hard to believe he was the same man who'd stalked out of her office last September and stalked back into it three weeks earlier.

"Stay, Demi." His voice was gentle, nearly tender. He was idly stroking her stomach, brushing lightly over her breasts. "I will need your help again in the morning."

She pretended to look suspicious. "With what?"

"You know, ironing my shirts, cooking me breakfast."

"Ha!"

"Okay, how about another massage? I'm liable to be stiff." He raised an eyebrow. "Of course most men wake up stiff…"

Demi groaned. "Saw that one a mile away."

"Stay. It's cold out. Might snow tomorrow."

"Really?"

"No. Stay."

She laughed, loving this crazy, intimate, funny time. "I shouldn't."

"I know."

Demi sighed, thinking about her career, her absolute adherence to the principles of her practice. How could she toss them aside so carelessly now? Just because Colin was hot?

No. Not just that. Because he was hot and she also suspected that he needed her, and she was starting to wonder if she needed some of what he could give her, too. At least right now. She wasn't the forever woman for him, and he wasn't the forever man for her, but...

"Stay?"

They'd have to talk about this, about him starting up with another therapist if he wanted to keep pushing her over the lines. The idea lightened her mood. She turned toward him, leaned over and kissed his forehead.

"I'll stay. But just this one time."

"Right, Demi." He chuckled in the darkness and put his arm all the way around her. "Just this one time."

8

MIRACLES COULD HAPPEN. Demi knew, because she managed to extract herself from Colin's bed that morning, give him another massage, more medication, help him get up and standing and leave the apartment without jumping him. What's more, he behaved remarkably well, not making more than a token protest at her insistence on impersonal contact.

Not to say this miracle had been easy to achieve. Demi had woken slowly, aware of him beside her as she had been at intervals all night long. The desire to wrap herself around him and fall back to sleep, or slowly stroke him awake to make love to her was so strong she had to force herself to lie still. Even then, she'd spent several minutes listening to Colin's slow breathing, reveling in that lovely feeling of waking up next to someone special. How special? She wasn't sure, couldn't shake the certainty that Colin was attracted to her because of what she was doing for him, and what she was bringing him at a low point in his life, not because of who she was.

Eventually, reason crowded in and forced her out of bed and into efficiency. But those had been really lovely minutes. And she'd guiltily enjoyed the taste of faux-domesticity between them, even if she'd gone firmly into caretaker role the second he woke.

Demi liked him. She really, really liked him. The way her body had responded to his touch…dangerous stuff. But more than that, she'd come to admire and respect his struggle. He was more than the babe-ogling high-fiving dude she originally thought. Much more than the bitter man he'd become when the accident so abruptly took his golden-boy status away.

She brought herself back to reality in her office and glanced at her watch. One more client before the day was over. Maybe she should call Colin and ask how he was doing? She wasn't sure what protocol to follow for clients she'd had sexual contact with because there wasn't any protocol like that. But she couldn't manage to regret what had happened. One slip, one night. If Colin wanted to keep some kind of sexual relationship going, he could find another PT. Otherwise, they'd keep on platonically as before. Either way, she wasn't going to start panting after him. She'd done plenty of panting last night in his bed, with his fingers on her and over her and into her. Oh, my God, she'd already had to duck into the bathroom once today and bring herself off thinking about it. All day today, seasonally cold in the upper forties, she'd been practically running a fever.

Her client was late, as he usually was. Fred Cranger had a rotator-cuff injury that she suspected had healed enough for him to be recovering on his own. But he was a top-notch hypochondriac and kept coming up with new pains in new places that needed her attention.

Shrug. Okay. Her time, his dime…

Fred finally showed up full of his usual apologies and phantom pain. After he left, she headed out for a run, then showered and got ready for a dinner date with Wesley, only checking her voice mail three or four dozen times.

Okay, not that many. But she did check too many times, even telling herself severely that he'd either call or not, and there was no point—

Phone.

She pounced on it, peering at the display screen.

Colin. *Yes.* Demi took a second to breathe so she wouldn't answer too eagerly.

Ready, set, go. "Hi, Colin, how are you feeling?"

"Not terrible."

Just his voice was making her hot. Two words, he'd said. Two! She was really in fantasy-lustland here. "Discouraged by the setback?"

"It's my own fault." Yes, he was discouraged.

"We'll get you back on track quickly. Setbacks are really common. Just keep thinking positive thoughts. And, uh, no more running today…"

He chuckled briefly. "Yeah, I promise."

"Good."

Awkward silence while they were probably both trying to calculate whether it was appropriate to keep the conversation professional or turn it personal. And right there was the reason Demi should have stayed out of his bed.

Except…she'd had so much fun in it.

"I was going to call you earlier but I was afraid you'd have wall-to-wall appointments today."

"I did, actually." She gave a stupid laugh over nothing funny.

More awkward silence.

This was crazy. They'd crossed a line they weren't supposed to, way before they knew each other well enough to, and now they were being exposed by the fact that they had nothing to say to each other.

"I want to see you, Demi."

Demi closed her eyes blissfully, pleasure zipping through

her body and settling in places it shouldn't. *Ohhh, my.* The way he'd said that, as if he couldn't possibly last more than a few hours without her...

Her eyes sprang open. Wait! Brilliant idea! "I'm having dinner tonight with my friend Wesley. Want to come along?"

"Friend?" He sounded skeptical.

"Uh-huh. You'd like him. We're meeting at Joe Bar at seven. I can drive if it's tough on your back." He agreed somewhat hesitantly, and made arrangements for Demi to pick him up at his place.

She ended the call feeling positively smug. Perfect. She could see Colin, but with a chaperone, making it clear this was not a date. *And* she could show him how one of her favorite people had come to terms with life after an injury that ended his competitive career.

First she needed to clear her brilliant idea with Wesley, though she was sure he wouldn't object. She dialed his number, feeling giddy at the prospect of seeing Colin again, even knowing she shouldn't be playing with this fire.

But...since when had she ever been sensible when it came to men? She had girlfriends who could pick and choose, this one, that one, this characteristic, that one. But Demi just felt. And when she felt that wild lust starting for someone, she knew it was trouble. Even throwing herself in that fire time after time and being repeatedly burned to a crisp hadn't diminished her optimism.

Silly girl.

At least she knew right from the outset that there was no happy ever after in the offing for her and Colin. Even if he did decide to find another PT and dated Demi for a while, eventually when he accepted what had happened to him, when he was ready to rejoin life pretty much as he'd known it, he'd naturally gravitate toward other types of women. Hadn't he said Stephanie was more like his beer-drinking sax teacher than his sedate mother? And that she ran marathons? Demi could just picture her. Tall, slender, athletic, big boobs, perfect white teeth, long wavy hair, a penchant for miniskirts and stilettos, which she could walk in like she was barefoot…

Everything quiet stay-at-home Demi wasn't.

Wesley picked up. "Hey, Demi."

"I thought I was going to go to voice mail there."

"I was in the shower. We still on tonight?"

"Absolutely, but…"

"Ye-e-es?"

"I've invited someone to join us."

"To join us? Well that sounds formal. Who is he?"

Demi frowned. "How did you know it's a he?"

"Because if it was a girlfriend you wouldn't be so nervous that you'd say something like, 'I've invited someone to join us.'"

She giggled. "Okay, okay. It's—"

"Colin Russo."

"What?" She pulled the phone from her ear and stared at it as if she was afraid it would bite. "Now you're freaking me out."

"Who else would it be?"

"Come on, there's no way you'd know that."

"Okay, okay, lucky guess. So who did the inviting?"

"He did." She grimaced. "Well, no, I did, sort of."

"Hmmm. Looking into my crystal ball I discover that he wanted to see you, but you said you were already seeing me, and then you invited him because it's—"

"*Where* did you put the surveillance equipment around here?" Demi noisily banged open a kitchen cabinet, pretending to look. "You must have installed it that night you were here eating Thai noodles."

"Nah. That one was easy. You would never initiate social time with a client, so the call must have come from him. And because you are a very ethical woman, and also scared to death of what you feel for him—"

"Now, wait a second."

He chuckled. "Congratulations, Demi! The unattainable hot guy wants you after all!"

She scoffed, feeling an unwelcome thrill. "Like that means anything."

"Okay, Ms. Low Self-esteem, why doesn't it?"

"Think about it. He's miserable, lonely, on the rebound from being dumped, and guess who's here to make him feel better?"

"Demi." Wesley made a sound of frustration. "Either you're hopeless or fishing for reassurance."

"As I recall, you were in the same situation he is. What did you do? You asked me out, too."

"Oh. Uh. Well." He cleared his throat. "So, um, still the same time and place tonight?"

She laughed. "Yes. And it would help if you'd find a nice, subtle way to talk about your new life postaccident and how rewarding it is. No sugarcoating, but some of the positives he can't see yet."

"Ah, Demi. My sweet devious saint. If that eases your conscience over the burning lust you feel for him, then yes, I'm happy to."

"Thanks, I think. See you soon." She hung up the phone, positively giddy. See? This wasn't a date. It was nothing like a date. This was a way Demi the PT could help her client navigate the rest of his life.

And what a damn fine job she was doing.

COLIN STEPPED OFF his building's elevator and went through the double doors into the chilly evening where he'd wait for Demi to pick him up. He was still moving carefully, but he'd come back from this latest injury a lot faster than he'd feared, thanks to big doses of anti-inflammatory meds and Demi's quick intervention. With her magic hands.

From what he remembered, his own hands had done some magic for her, too. *Man*. That was some unbelievably sexy stuff. He hadn't stopped thinking about it since he woke up this morning, to find Demi transformed back into brisk PT Anderson, a persona that had started amusing rather than annoying him.

Because he'd discovered PT Anderson's secret. Under that cool professional exterior, she was one of the hottest, most sensual women he'd ever met. The juxtaposition drove him wild. How he'd managed to lie still watching her come, he had no idea. Fear of pain must be a more powerful driving force than he thought. That, and the certainty that if he'd pushed their sexual contact any further, she'd have bolted.

Her initial reluctance, her gradual arousal, her climax— he might as well have a video of the event, it was so clear in his mind. Not to mention he'd played that mental video over and over and over, hearing her gasps, her moans, feeling her soft skin and her wetness under his fingers. She'd opened completely, lost all inhibition, become a totally sexual creature responding to him.

He wanted more. He wanted it all. He wanted to make love to her in every possible position in every possible location that didn't get them arrested. Starting tonight.

On cue, a car pulled into the circle in front of his building, driven by a dark-haired woman. A bright yellow car. A bright yellow Volkswagen Beetle.

Good God. First he'd break his back getting into that toy, and then it would turn him bisexual.

She pulled up in front of him, grinning, and he forgot all about the ridiculous car, and everything else that his consciousness might be trying to register, because his passionate mystery woman was here. Tonight she wore a turquoise scoop-neck top that made her pale skin even more enticing, and set off her dark hair in a stark and striking contrast. Her lips were a maroon shade that emphasized their beautiful shape and made him realize with a sudden shock that he'd never kissed her.

He would tonight.

"How do you expect me to get in that tiny excuse for a vehicle and ever be able to walk again?"

"There's tons of room. You'll be amazed."

He wasn't sure *amazed* was the right word, but he did fit comfortably, and he liked the intimacy of being in a car with her, even though his masculinity was as threatened by the yellow bug as it was not being behind the wheel on a date with a woman.

Another surprise awaited him: Demi drove like a NASCAR professional. Totally unexpected, but it only added to her allure. A shy woman who in certain areas liked to live on the edge. The road. And the bedroom.

They reached the bar a short time later—certainly shorter than if he'd been driving. Parking was kind to them; she found a space around the corner on Broadway and they walked to tree-lined Roy Street. Joe Bar turned out not to be the hip bar he'd expected, but a neighborhood coffee shop that served beer, wine and food along with various versions of java. It made more sense that Demi would be drawn to a place like this, friendly and low-key, with green walls, dark wood and enough paintings to make Colin suspect it doubled as gallery space.

Her friend Wesley was a tall, good-looking guy with dark hair, blue eyes and an athletic build, who greeted Demi with obvious affection. Colin kept his expression pleasant, hiding the jab of jealousy that sneaked up on him. Good move, because when Demi introduced them and they shook hands, Wesley's eyes were assessing, but friendly, not at all threatened or threatening.

They ordered sandwiches, crepes—Joe Bar's specialty—and beers, chatting easily about a movie Wesley had seen recently with his girlfriend, then about the Seahawks' season. Upstairs, they found a table and arranged themselves around it.

"So I guess I don't need to ask how you and Demi met." Wesley gestured between them with his beer.

"Same way you and I did." Demi smiled at Colin, and turned back to Wes.

"That right?" Colin didn't like thinking of her hands all over Wesley's impressive body, so he decided Demi had treated him for something wrong with his foot, and that he had hideous feet.

"Wes had a traumatic brain injury."

"Damn." Colin sucked air in through his teeth, immediately regretting the childish foot joke. "I can't imagine there's any other kind."

Wesley chuckled. "No, you don't hear about many 'pleasurable brain injuries.'"

"How did it happen?" He lowered his beer. "If you don't want to talk about it…"

"Car accident." Wesley toasted Demi, eyes softening. "She got me walking again."

"You couldn't *walk?*" Colin tried to imagine his body betraying him to such an extent, or the rage and impotence that kind of disability could engender. He'd had a baby boo-boo in comparison.

"I couldn't move much at all right after it happened. Amazing how you come back from that shit."

"Incredible." If Wesley hadn't told him, Colin never

would have known, though he had noticed a slight shuffle in Wesley's stride. "I bet that took a lot of hard work."

"Yeah." He said it offhandedly, but the expression on Demi's face told him how much Wesley had suffered. "You get used to it. The hardest part was not being able to run anymore."

"You ran?" Colin dragged his attention away from the gorgeous sight of Demi's neck curving down to the low scoop of her top, from which peeked two beautiful breasts his hands had had the intense pleasure of exploring the night before.

"Wes was a marathoner." Demi's voice was quietly matter-of-fact, which was somehow more horrifying than if she'd been pouring on the sympathy. "New York, Boston, all the big ones. He took fourth in Minneapolis three years ago."

"No kidding." Colin took two seconds to be impressed before the obvious hit him. *Was* a marathoner. The accident took that away. His beer suddenly tasted sour. He dug into his sandwich and could barely taste it.

"And you did Ironmen?" Wesley asked.

Did Ironmen. He and Wesley had lots in common. "Yeah."

"I'm sorry." Like Demi, Wes spoke quietly, but it was clear he knew what Colin had suffered, and for once Colin didn't mind the sympathy. "It sucks. No way around it."

Demi was looking at him expectantly, and it hit him why she'd arranged this little evening. Not for herself. She'd done this for him. So he could talk to someone who knew exactly what he was going through.

Part of him was immediately pissed off. She'd manipulated him into this.

Part of him was immediately hurt. She hadn't included him so she could get near him again as soon as possible. She was still treating him. PT Anderson.

Part of him was humbled and pleased. This wasn't part

of her job. She wasn't getting paid for this. She'd gone out of her way to help him in a very personal way. Maybe she did this for all her clients, but he doubted it.

Okay. He took a deep breath. Showing weakness wasn't his strong suit, but he couldn't repay Demi for this kindness by being rude. "How did you come back?"

"Part of me never will. Facing that was the hardest. And because I did come back so far so fast, it's still a battle, because I keep thinking, well, why not keep improving? But brain damage is brain damage and I've got it. I won't run again. But there were some really dark days when I thought I wouldn't even walk again. So I try to be grateful and I do succeed a lot of the time. It's hard to keep that perspective. It's doubly hard to rewire your whole life's focus."

"No kidding."

"And there's that other shit that happens, which people don't tell you about. Even Demi."

"What?" She pretended outrage. "Are you implying I'm somehow imperfect?"

"Of course not." Wesley grinned and briefly stroked her back. Colin managed not to grit his teeth, but he didn't love the easy, intimate way Wesley touched her. That was starting to feel like his job.

"What other stuff?" He had a feeling he knew.

"The way people disappear. Friends you used to train with. You realize that's all you had in common with some of them. And for others, you've come to represent their worst nightmare and they can't handle the change. My girlfriend dumped me. And it was years before my mother could look at me without bawling."

Colin nodded, unable to speak. He was angry on Wesley's behalf and every other poor sucker whose life kicked him in the teeth. And he was suddenly and savagely angry at Stephanie, who ran from his broken body to Nick's still-whole one, as if triathlons were all she valued about him.

"Relax, Colin." A hand landed on his arm, and he realized he was holding his beer in a death grip. "Breathe. I don't want you stuck back in bed."

It took a second for him to focus on Demi and realize what she'd just said, but when it registered, his anger fled, and he gave her a slow, intimate grin. "You don't?"

There. A blush the color of roses. He loved doing that to her. Especially when it was a flush of intense pleasure instead of embarrassment, the way it had been last night.

Wesley was grinning between them, but stopped abruptly when he met Colin's eyes. Not manly to be caught gooping over another guy's budding relationship. Colin respected that. "Sorry to have gone on about the head injury, Colin. I don't mean to be a downer."

"You can't be," Colin said. "I'm living similar stuff every day."

"There are silver linings, as Demi no doubt has told you."

"Oh, only about four million times."

Demi glared at him. "Hey, it helps *and* it's true."

"She's right." Wesley shrugged. "You might not be there yet, but life does get better. You find out who your friends are. You find out who you are. Marathons are what I did, not who I was."

Colin quirked an eyebrow, not sure he was buying all the happy-ending crap. He still couldn't totally let go of his dream of Hawaii. Maybe he never would be able to. "Who are you now?"

"A teacher. A coach. A good friend. A better man."

In spite of his cynicism, Colin couldn't help a flash of hopefulness. "So you're telling me you prefer your life now?"

"In some ways, absolutely. I'm less selfish. I'm more about helping other people, less about what I can do for myself. I discovered I love kids. I discovered I want to be married and have some. Before, it was just about pushing harder, going faster. I like myself better now."

"I like you better, too." Demi grinned at him, then squeezed Colin's forearm. "You think *you* were a pain in the ass…"

He pretended deep offense. "No, I absolutely do not. What are you talking about?"

She snorted. God, she was beautiful. The longer he was around her the more he wanted her all to himself. "Let's just say Wesley made you look like an amateur."

Wesley nodded. "I was pretty angry."

"You were pretty badly injured." Colin lifted his beer in a respectful salute. "I just fell off my bike. Any kid can do that."

"Hey, your injury is a tough one, Colin." Demi plonked her beer down on the table. His heart turned over. Not only because he really wanted to kiss her, but because she always supported him, in her quiet way, didn't let him put himself down or get discouraged. Maybe there was something to that positive-thinking crap.

Demi was a good person. And he really wanted her tonight.

They switched to lighter topics, talking about the upcoming winter, skiing plans that couldn't happen for either guy, alternate suggestions that went from the sublime—a cruise in the Bahamas—to the ridiculous—building igloos up in the mountains.

Not long after 9:00 p.m. the staff started clearing up. Colin wanted to cheer. The place closed early, hallelujah. He'd really enjoyed meeting Wesley, but he was dying to get Demi alone.

They said good-night outside the café, and Colin and Demi walked to the sunshine-yellow abomination that was her car.

"How's your back holding up?"

"Not bad. A little sore. I'm due for more meds." He slid her a sideways grin. "And a long, slow massage would really help."

"Uh-huh." She unlocked the car. "Make an appointment."

"Okay." He climbed in gingerly. "How about my place in ten minutes? Five the way you drive?"

"I'll have to check my schedule."

Her reply was so unexpected he was stunned into silence. Horny silence. She wasn't going to fight him?

The idea made him fold his hands in his lap to hide the evidence of his…anticipation. "Thanks for introducing me to Wesley."

"You're welcome." She glanced at him before she tore out of their parking place and roared down the street. "He's a good guy."

"You were trying to help me."

"Well, yes. Did it work?"

"It did. Not that I had any doubts I'd make it to the other side of this, but…" He shrugged. "Okay, maybe once in a while."

"It's impossible not to doubt."

He nodded, bemused that he could show weakness around her. When had he met someone who simply accepted him as he was? To his parents, he was always the weird kid who didn't march to his father's military drum, a creative dreamer of a boy, more into moving his body than moving his mind, but sensitive and not a joiner. He fit no type his dad could relate to, so it followed Colin was the wrong type. His brothers and his father joined everything that would take them—clubs, military branches, associations, everything—while Colin was in the basement playing his sax, making his knives or alone out on the road, running to exhaustion.

"As I said, I appreciate that you arranged for me to meet Wesley tonight." He sighed loudly and clasped his hands behind his head. "But I kind of hoped you'd invited me because you couldn't wait to see me again."

"I didn't *mind* seeing you again." The look she shot him this time was just shy of flirtatious. "Because I was worried about your physical condition."

"That's it?"

"Oh, yes." Her next glance inched closer to sexual invitation. "What other reason would there be?"

"Can't think of a thing." He wouldn't share his "physical condition" at the moment. A hard-on from contemplating what they might do tonight. "It's nice seeing you in something other than black, Demi. You look beautiful."

"Hmm."

"Hmm?" He reached over and put his hand to the back of her neck, loving the feel of her skin and the softness of her hair cascading over his fingers. "You *are* beautiful."

"You *are* delusional." She put her foot down and they shot ahead, nearly at the exit for his building already.

"In a hurry?"

"No. Why?"

He laughed, massaging the muscles at the base of her neck. "You drive like you're desperate."

She kept her gaze straight ahead. "Not desperate, no."

"I think I am."

This time he earned a frowning glance. "I am pretty sure I don't want to ask this, but for what?"

"To figure out what this is between us." He laid his hand alongside her cheek. "And what we're planning to do about it."

9

WHAT WERE THEY planning to do about it?

Demi took Roosevelt Way to Forty-seventh Street. At Forty-seventh, she'd go left, left again and be at Colin's place.

And then what?

Maybe she already knew the answer to his question, though she'd responded only with a joke about pleading the fifth. Certainly being with him was what she wanted. But not if Colin was going to keep seeing her as a therapist. That one night they spent together had pushed her ethical boundaries to the max. Demi could lose her license if it came out that she'd had sexual relations with a client.

She was just having a hard time seeing how making Colin come so hard he yelled for mercy was wrong in any way.

It was important they talked this out and that both of them were clear on what was at stake, legally, emotionally and, with his back only barely recovering, physically.

How did she get herself into this situation? Anyone in her right mind would drop Colin off, say good-night and drive home.

But around Colin, Demi wasn't entirely sure she was ever in her right mind.

"You can park in the visitor lot there." He pointed to the one opposite the building's entrance.

Demi came to a stop, neither in the lot nor by the entrance. *"Am* I parking?"

"Yes."

"You've decided this, huh."

"Yes."

She turned to him in the dim light of the car's interior. "And what, then I'm coming upstairs with you?"

"Yes."

"For…"

"A private tour of my knife collection." He grinned mischievously. "I want to make one for you. You can tell me what type you'd like."

"More gifts?" She shook her head, clucking her tongue.

"Well, gee." Colin was all innocence. "Making knives again is part of my therapy, right?"

"Hmm."

A car pulled up behind her. Demi turned into the visitor lot, chose a space and killed the engine. "I think we need to talk about—"

"Upstairs." He opened the door and got out into air that had a distinctly wintery bite. "If I stay in your car any longer I'll start wanting to wear pink."

Demi sat for two beats, then sighed and got out. Colin was striding well, tall, straight and almost graceful. He was nearly at the entrance when she caught up to him. He gallantly held open the door to the building's lobby, dominated by a table on which sat an immense dried flower arrangement that looked as if it had done plenty of time there.

In the elevator they were saved from awkward silence by a woman on her cell phone loudly discussing every detail of a so-so date the entire way up. She was still talking when they got off on Colin's floor.

"Remind me not to ask her out." He shuddered, then unlocked his apartment door and pushed it open to let Demi go first. "Home sweet home."

"Thank you." She waited until he'd closed the door, before confronting him, hands on her hips. "Colin, we need to talk about what's going—"

"Let me pour us a drink first." He grinned when she shot him a look. "You like cognac?"

She was taken aback. Her dad had loved the stuff, let Demi taste it now and then, but she didn't know anyone her age who enjoyed it. "I do, actually."

"Good." He moved into his kitchen, reached up to take a bottle out of the cabinet above his refrigerator.

"You're moving well."

"You think so, huh." He winked at her. "I have a damn good physical therapist."

"Thank you." She watched him pour out two good measures of brandy into modest-sized snifters, surprised at how comfortable she was, even though she generally felt a combination of annoyance and unease in fancy condos. And she wasn't sure she should be in Colin's in the first place.

"Let's go in the living room?"

"Sure." She followed him and sat on the couch, half dismayed, half pleased when he sat next to her. Close.

This was going to make it hard to keep her logical mind on full alert for their discussion.

"Cheers." He clinked his glass with hers, looking steadily into her eyes, flustering her further. She watched him sip, watched his very fine mouth savoring the liqueur before he swallowed.

Mmm, yes. Flustered. She raised her glass in self-defense.

The sweet, fiery taste was warming, elegant and comforting. "Very good."

"Glad you like it." He took her hand, held it idly, rubbing his fingers over hers. "So talk to me, Demi. Tell me what reasons you're cooking up for why you can't be with me tonight. Why you can't come into my bedroom and let me undress you, then touch every part of your body. Why it's such a bad idea to invite you to touch every part of mine until neither of us can stand waiting anymore and we give each other enough pleasure to make us scream."

Demi half laughed, half gasped, cheeks hot, chest hot, and everything female about her very, very hot. "You're not playing fair."

"Oh, and by the way?" He toasted her with his snifter. "You're fired."

That got through. Barely. "What?"

"Yup." He was irritatingly cheerful. "You're no longer my physical therapist."

"Wait, are you serious? You're firing me?"

He nodded.

She was totally confused now. Wasn't this what she wanted, for him to make this exact decision?

And yet, as she sat here with him now, it hit her that treating Colin's injuries, helping unlock the man from the bitter cage he was in...that had come to mean a lot to her. And obviously nothing to him if he was happily ditching that relationship in order to get laid. Any woman could help him with that.

"Is there any other way we can sleep together?"

Demi drank more brandy, then drained the glass, swallowing convulsively, feeling demeaned. "No."

"Then that's it. We're clear." His smile died at the look on her face. "Uh...okay, no, we're not clear."

"You're leaving therapy so we can have sex tonight."

"Yes, exactly." He looked hopeful, then gradually more and more pained. "Okay, this is one of those times when I'm being a clueless guy, isn't it. Because I thought you wanted this, too."

"I do."

"So…"

Right. Male logic. Made sense to him. And outwardly to her. But inwardly… She couldn't talk to him about her reaction because it would mean admitting more vulnerability than she cared to.

"It feels as if my body is worth more to you than my… expertise." To her horror, her voice emerged shaky instead of assured.

"Whoa, Demi. No, that's not what this is about." He took her shoulders, tipped her face up to his, warm and concerned. Where had Cranky Colin gone? She'd helped bring this part of him back to life. What would happen to him without her? "I gave this a lot of thought. You're the best PT I've ever had, and I'm not giving you up lightly. But our sessions in that massage room were pure torture. Your hands on me were torture. Then after the other night, when I finally got my hands on you…"

He blew out a silent whistle.

She nodded. "It was hard on me, too."

"Oh, you think so?" He was smugly skeptical.

Demi bristled. *"Yes."*

"Sorry. When it comes to being hard, trust me, I win."

He could make her laugh even when she was anxious and confused. Maybe the more appropriate question was the reverse of one she'd asked already—what would happen to *her* without *him?* "One more thing."

"Go ahead."

"What happens after we do this tonight? We're finished and you rehire me? Or we're done?"

"No. No. Not like that." He dragged his hand down his face. "Obviously I did this all wrong. Here it is, then. I want us to hang out, Demi. I want to ask you to dinner sometimes, or to go biking or eventually running together. We can go to jazz concerts, ball games, movies. Maybe we can go virtual-necklace shopping. Or hey, I know, sit at your place and *knit* together."

Her laughter had a slightly raw edge. "That sounds way hot."

"Bottom line, I don't just want you tonight. I'll want you tomorrow, too. More than once, likely. And the day after that and the day after that..."

She smiled at his eagerness, more confused than happy, and not sure why that was the case. His view was clear. His little speech—of remarkable length for Colin—put to rest her fears that he was rebounding, vulnerable, and Demi just happened to be there. He didn't sound like a man on his way to falling for her. He just wanted company as he went through his recovery. Maybe that would be all right, and they could—

"Stop." He put gentle fingers to her forehead, gazed earnestly into her face. "You're overthinking this."

God, his eyes were beautiful. "You're right."

"It's not that complicated."

His mouth was beautiful, too. "It's not really uncomplicated, either, Colin, because—"

"Shh. Only positive thoughts." His hand moved down her face, his fingers brushed across her mouth, making it tingle.

Then his lips took their place.

Ohhh, my. The second his mouth touched hers she realized they'd never kissed. And oh, how fabulous it was. Lingering, gentle kisses, tasting, tempting her to want more.

"You fired me." She tilted her head to let him explore,

under her ear, down her jaw, then down the length of her neck. "That's never happened to me before."

"I guess no one has wanted you as much as I do."

His words gave her a brief thrill. Yes, he wanted her. Not only in his bed tonight, but again and into the future, as companion, friend, lover... For a time, anyway.

She was still trying to wrap her brain around her reaction to that one, but it had started shutting down functions except pleasure receptors, so she might have to let the concept lie for now.

"Demi." He spoke against her lips.

"Mmm."

"Would you like to move into my bedroom?"

"Well. As a physical therapist, though no longer yours, I would advise you not to try anything athletic on your couch. So yes."

"I'll keep that in mind." He got up, only slightly stiff, and held out his hand.

"So you're not going to show me your knives?"

He chuckled. "How about in the morning."

"I'm spending the night?"

"Yes."

"You're bossy, you know that?"

"Yes."

Then he was kissing her again, long, heady kisses that made something inside her melt and harden at the same time. Which didn't sound possible, but that was exactly how it felt. Maybe it would always be that way between them. The more she felt, the more she'd want to protect herself.

But tonight...she was going to give herself over to this physical experience with him, because they both wanted it, and there was no longer any reason not to, though a court of law might not entirely agree, since she was going to be in bed with him roughly fifteen minutes after their professional relationship ended.

Demi had a feeling Colin wouldn't tell the authorities. She wouldn't, either.

"I'm bossy, too," she announced.

"No kidding."

"And as your former PT, I'm going to insist that we proceed tonight in a way that will put you at minimal risk of further injury."

"Oh?" He backed them up until the bed stopped him. "And what does this plan entail?"

She planted a finger in the center of his chest and pushed gently. "You. Naked."

"So far I like it."

"On your back on the bed, with a pillow under your knees, not moving at all. No matter what I do to you."

"Uh…" He pretended to look alarmed. "I *think* I like it. Do I? You're just bossy, right? Not a sado-dominatrix?"

"Not." She pushed harder on his chest, until he sat on the edge of the bed. "But I strongly suggest you do what I say."

"Or else?" He ran his hands up the outsides of her thighs, clasped her around the waist and nuzzled between her breasts.

She smiled, caressed his head. "Or else you might hurt yourself. And then we wouldn't get to try this again for weeks."

He let go of her abruptly, looked up in mock-panic. "Don't say that."

Demi burst into more giggles. This man was such a far cry from the sour cynic who'd first needed her help. She liked him more and more. "Let's get you out of these clothes."

"Let's." He raised his shirt over his head, and even though she'd seen that torso naked before, touched most every inch of it, she still took in a breath of pleasure at the sight.

"You are a stunningly built man, Colin Russo."

"You." He spread his knees and hugged her between them. "Are so right."

Again she laughed, pushing him gently back on the bed. "Down, ego boy."

He hauled himself up until his whole body was on the mattress, and slid the pillow under his knees as instructed, to help align his back optimally. "I'm down."

"Pants, too."

He pulled them off. "They're down."

"And…" She quirked an eyebrow and pointed to his boxer briefs, snapping her fingers, trying to look stern. My God, the man was a sight. She'd seen parts of him under the sheet while massaging him, but the sight of that torso connecting so gracefully to his gorgeously muscled legs…mmm.

"I'm shy." He was already pulling them off.

"Yeah, I can see that."

"Can you?" He was laughing at her now, half-erect, his penis a thing of awe-inspiring power and beauty.

"Oh, my."

"All yours, Demi." His grin took on a tenderness that made her lower her eyes to collect herself. This wasn't about love, this was about hanging out. And my goodness, was he ever.

"Remember, don't move." She backed up a few steps, holding herself straight, the way she'd learned in the ballet class her mother made her and her sister take. Predictably, Carrie had been a gazelle, Demi a duck. But not tonight. Tonight she was Colin's most fabulous sexual fantasy.

She forced herself to meet his dark gaze again; this time she was ready and the contact no longer overwhelmed her.

This was her show. She might not be one of the red-hot babes he usually dated, but he wanted her, and he was going to get the best she had to offer.

Grateful for the bracing brandy, she grasped the hem of her top and eased it up and off, letting the material muss her hair, not bothering to smooth it back off her face.

"Oh, Demi." He was holding still as instructed, watching intently.

She smiled at him sensually, unhooked her bra and brought her forearms close, letting it slide off while her breasts pushed together in an offering meant to impress.

If the way his eyes bugged out of his head was any indication, it did. And he was no longer riding at half-mast, but full.

Gaining confidence, she drew her elbows back, wet her index finger and painted circles around and over each nipple until a whimper sounded from the bed.

"Don't move," she said sharply.

"You're killing me."

"Am I?" She pretended surprise, put her hands to the stretch waistband of her skirt and eased it off, rocking her hips side to side. "Make sure you're relaxing totally. You don't want to strain—"

"My *back's* not in danger of straining." He gestured to his rigid cock, thick and golden, his balls drawn tight underneath. "But if you keep doing that, I might have to get a sling for my—"

"Shh. Arm down. No moving."

He groaned. "Yes, ma'am."

She stood before him, naked except for her underpants, and caressed her stomach, undulating her hips, then dipped a hand under the soft cotton of her panties.

Sharp intake of breath from the bed.

"You like this? Me, too, Colin." She spoke in a low, languid voice. "It feels amazing. Very warm. Very soft. And getting kind of slippery."

He responded with something that sounded like "ungh." Demi felt like purring. Modern man reduced to caveman essentials.

"Do you want to see me?"

Another grunt, head nodding, face pained.

She moved the underpants down, then stood quietly, letting him look.

He struggled to sit; she held up her hand. "Stop."

His body fell obediently back onto the mattress. "Help... me..."

She giggled, ruining her seductive-siren routine, but who cared? Colin had responded beyond her wildest dreams, and she no longer felt the need to compete with whatever female she thought he wanted most.

A few steps and she was at the edge of the bed. She climbed up, prowling like a cat about to pounce, pressing kisses to his knees, thighs, hip bones, and then finally, to the beautiful, hard-soft length of his cock, inhaling his male scent.

"Mmm." She ran her tongue from base to tip, took the first inch into her mouth and played there with lips, tongue and teeth. Grasping him gently, she fingered his balls, until his hands curled into fists, and his breath was nearly painful to listen to.

"Demi..."

"Condom?"

"In the nightstand drawer."

"Excellent." Demi retrieved one and rolled it over his erection, lifted her leg to straddle him and positioned herself directly over his penis, where she paused to heighten the anticipation. Then, closing her eyes, she sank one slow inch, thighs starting to tremble as his cock touched her, nudged, pushed just inside her.

"Oh, my."

"Demi…"

Then she made the mistake. She opened her eyes and caught his. In seconds, the most extraordinary wave of emotion tumbled over her. She froze, unable to handle the rush that nearly stopped her breath. What was happening? Was she having an anxiety attack?

His hands landed on her hips; he pushed up, and the icy block broke. She sank down onto him as a grateful moan echoed from his mouth, and they moved together, slowly, gracefully, until his arms came up around her and he pulled her down on top of him. In that position, she could only tip her pelvis back and forth, which ground her clitoris against him. Hearing his quickening breath, she knew he was as turned on as she was. Good. This was safely carnal and hot as hell.

She spoke too soon. He turned her face to his, and keeping up the slow, incendiary rhythm of their lovemaking, he touched his mouth to hers. The kiss went on and on, tongues tasting, retreating, lips fitting, refitting, and all the while the glorious friction of his slow slide inside her.

Their faces separated, their eyes locked again, and she was drawn into the depths of his gaze to a degree that terrified and elated her all at once.

This was too much. Way too much. Too intense and too sweet and not at all what was called for here. This was their first time. They hardly knew each other. They were here for hot sex and good laughs.

She lifted off him and began a strong, pumping rhythm he responded to by closing his eyes and urging her on with his hands.

"Yes. That's… Demi… Oh, yes." His breathing became

harsh; his fingers dug into her ass. Her vagina was on fire around him, and she could feel every inch of him inside her; every thrust pulled on her clitoris, building her higher and higher. Sweat broke out on her body. She felt herself gathering for her climax.

"Colin," she whispered. "I'm going to come. Now. It's starting."

He groaned and pushed up with one furious thrust, then blew air harshly through his teeth. She felt him pulsing inside her at the same time that she surrendered to her own ecstasy.

Afterward, she lay on him, fighting a rush of tenderness. *Do not make more of this than it is, Demi.* This wasn't like her. She was perfectly able to date men casually even when sex was part of the equation.

The problem here was that she'd invested too much emotion in Colin's recovery. So it was a damn good thing he'd fired her. Everything she was feeling right now, no matter how intense, no matter how lovely and how wonderful, she had to back away from, slowly—no sudden moves. Because with Colin in this odd place in his life right now, and her emotional overinvestment in his treatment, nothing either of them felt could be trusted.

10

UH-OH. BONNIE KEPT the polite smile pasted on her face, aware that Don had just asked her something. She desperately hit a mental Rewind to see if she could retrieve any of what he'd been talking about.

Nothing. Her panic grew. It wasn't the first time this had happened, and it was inexcusably rude.

They were sitting in her kitchen on a Friday night, sharing a bottle of wine. She'd lit candles for the table, had brought up a small bouquet of mixed sweetheart roses for the centerpiece, set the stage for a romantic evening between two people who still hadn't become lovers, though not for lack of Bonnie trying, and...

Once again, she couldn't keep her mind on what he was saying.

This was not a good sign.

"Ask me again, Don?"

He looked startled, then confused. "Was there something wrong with the way I asked?"

"No. No. Oh no, of course not." She blushed, shaking her head too many times. Don didn't deserve this. He was incredibly sweet, attractive, intelligent, funny and sophisticated. On paper, perfect. So what was wrong with her? "I just—"

"Wasn't listening."

She didn't know what to say, how to fix it. She couldn't lie. Her misery grew. "I'm sorry."

"Nah, it's okay." He took a sip of wine, put the glass down exactly in the center of his napkin as he always did, making Bonnie want to knock it askew just to see what would happen. Would he have a panic attack? Become enraged? Or simply cease to exist in a small puff of smoke? "I kind of go on sometimes."

"I'm distracted tonight. Sorry. Some complicated stuff at the store."

"Yeah? Can I help?"

Sure, get me out of debt so I don't have to give up the shop. She'd gotten a letter from the bank, and it was not friendly how's-it-going? correspondence. Bonnie had spent too long in denial, too long telling herself not to worry about her financial situation, that something would work out. It hadn't. "Don, you are so sweet, thanks, but no, it's my burden."

"Okay."

She drank more of her wine, more than she should, especially since Don had been sipping his and she'd been slugging back healthy gulps. About three inches left in the bottle; Bonnie was afraid she'd had most of it. But she was on edge tonight. It was time she really faced that she was going to lose her store, that she'd have to leave Come to Your Senses and find somewhere to start over. Where would she go? What would she do? The possibilities frightened and exhilarated her—in a manic, unnatural way—and made her extrasensitized, as if everything around her had become more meaningful and more intense.

Which also meant little things about Don that didn't deserve to be annoying were annoying her. He'd given up so easily when she said she didn't need help, hadn't asked what was wrong or if she wanted to talk about it. Which was ridiculous because he was probably being respectful of her privacy, assuming that if Bonnie wanted to talk, she would.

Seth would have understood that she needed to vent and he would have listened, then offered a solution, which she'd either accept or reject. But at least she'd end up feeling heard and cared for and therefore stronger.

She sucked down more wine, aware the comparison was unfair. Seth had been a friend first, then a lover and intimate friend, and then a friend again for the five years since they'd broken up.

Except…from the beginning he'd been remarkably tuned in to what she needed, even if he was clueless about understanding what *he* needed.

"We should go to the jazz festival one night."

"Oh." Bonnie nodded, thinking it would have been nice before he suggested the date if he'd asked whether she enjoyed jazz.

She didn't.

Mood plummeting further, she drained her glass. Sometimes alcohol gave her a lift, made her chatty and energized, and sometimes it plunged her into a miserable stupor that was very difficult to dig herself out of.

Today was apparently going to be one of the bad times. She should stop now, while she was only mildly behind.

Instead, she poured herself more.

"Whoa." Don chuckled uncomfortably. "Slow down there, girl."

Bonnie gritted her teeth. If he'd said, "This isn't like you. Why are you drinking so much?" that would have been nice. A simple "Hey, what's wrong?" would have worked, too. Pretty much anything but "Whoa, slow down there, girl" as if he was talking to his horse.

Poor Don. She was not being fair to him.

Or maybe she finally was being fair to herself. She didn't love this man. She never would. Her initial attraction and optimism had paled. When was the last time she went out with a guy several times, had been in his apartment and he in hers, and still hadn't slept with him? They'd made out some, but Don never took the bait, and by now she really couldn't care either way.

That wasn't a good sign, either.

"Sorry, Don, I'm having a rough night, I guess."

"I guess." He chuckled again, a humorless cackle that made it clear he was not amused.

Bonnie's teeth could conceivably crack. No sympathy. No empathy.

Don was a dud.

No, no, he'd be fine for the right woman. One who didn't need a deep physical and emotional connection. Bonnie wasn't that woman. It would be kinder to end it now.

Instead of panic, the idea of being free gave her a jolt of excitement.

Then panic.

So? She'd been single plenty in her life. And there was always Seattledates.com to search for someone who suited her better. Crazy to think she'd be lucky enough to hit the jackpot on the first try. Unless she left Seattle. Unless starting over included a complete change. The possibility instantly appealed, though she knew better than to make any major decisions when she was a tipsy disaster of a person.

In any case, first things first. She blew out a breath, then turned to face the music, who was looking thoughtful. "Don, I've been thinking..."

"Yeah, me, too."

She blinked in surprise. "About what?"

"Us."

"Oh. Me, too."

"Good." He looked vastly relieved. It would be so wonderful if he dumped her right now. Sad, bittersweet—it was always bittersweet when the hopes that rode along with a brand-new relationship were crushed. But if he did the dumping then she didn't have to.

"Go ahead, Don." She figuratively crossed her fingers. Now that she'd made the decision to break up, she wanted the whole thing over and done.

He put his hand over hers, his face wreathed in worry. *No, Don, no worries. Pull that plug!* "I was thinking…I should spend the night tonight."

Oh. Crap.

"I am *really* attracted to you, Bonnie." He trailed his fingers up her arm to her shoulder, then curled his hand in the curve of her neck. "I think you're totally hot. And we've waited long enough."

She sat stiffly. It was as if someone had just lifted her blindfold. "*I* should spend the night." "*I'm* really attracted." "*We've* waited enough." No asking how she felt about it or what she wanted, and not seeming to care that she'd already told him she was upset and distracted by bad news tonight.

"Where do I fit into this?"

He looked startled. "What do you mean? I'm saying I want us to have sex tonight."

She laughed, although nothing about this was funny. "I meant what about what I want to do tonight?"

He dragged his chair closer, put his hand on her thigh and smiled earnestly. "You just have to tell me, Bonnie, and we'll do it."

She groaned and dropped her head back in despair, eyes closed. He thought she was already mentally in bed with him, working out sexual positions. A spectacular miscommunication.

"God, Bonnie." He practically lunged at her, burying his face in her neck and sucking as if she had a snakebite he needed to treat.

"Don!" She shoved him away. "What are you *doing?*"

He pulled back immediately, looking stunned. "I'm trying to make love to you."

"But I haven't said I wanted you to."

"You dropped your head back and moaned like you were getting turned on." He was clearly annoyed now. "What, I have to wait for written permission?"

"No, that's not what I meant. I just…" She sighed. "Look, we're not on the same page here at all."

"What's not to understand? I want to make love to you."

"And I want to break up with you."

Silence.

Half an hour later, Bonnie closed the door behind Don, who clumped down the hall, raging loudly.

Instead of feeling relief and doing a happy dance around her kitchen, she burst into tears, threw herself on the living-room couch and began what she was afraid would be one of those endless cries that stopped for a few minutes, only to start again.

A knock on her door.

"Go away."

"Bonnie, let me in."

Seth. She lifted her head, eyes streaming. "Go away."

"Let me in."

"Leave me alone. Go write another YouTube hit or something."

"Let me in or I'll break the damn door down."

"You're not going to break the damn door down."

"I'm going to try. Let me in."

"For God's sake." She stomped over to the door, sniffling and wiping her eyes, whipped open the lock and whirled around immediately so she could stomp back to the couch, mumbling about what complete and utter poo-balls men were, and why did she have to want one at all, and maybe she would do better turning gay or giving her life to Jesus.

Seth burst into the apartment behind her. "What happened here?"

"What do you mean what happened here?" She stopped stomping, but she didn't feel like talking to him or anyone.

Wait, yes, she did.

No, she didn't. She just wanted her couch.

No, she didn't.

She started crying again.

Arms came around her shoulders; Seth's wide chest pressed against her back, rocking her. "Hey there, what's going on?"

She shook her head.

"I heard Don crashing out of here sounding angry, so I came down the hall and heard you crying." His arms tightened around her. "He better not have—"

"He didn't." She sniffed, wiping her eyes again. "I dumped him."

Seth went very still behind her. "Why?"

Bonnie shrugged, sniffed again. "He wasn't right for me, what do you think?"

"I think you need a tissue."

She did. Seth knew she'd be better discussing what happened after she'd blown her nose and calmed down. But he'd want to listen, he'd want to know and he'd care. Why couldn't he be right for her when he was so…right for her?

"Here." He pushed the tissue at her, stood watching her dry her face and blow her nose, tall, reassuring, hands on his hips, gray eyes narrow with concern.

"Thanks." She started into the kitchen. "Want some wine?"

"Sure. What are you pouring?"

"Wine." She hid a near-hysterical giggle. Mr. Vintage-Snob would be rolling his eyes. "Red."

"What *kind* of red? Cabernet? Merlot? Shiraz?"

"I dunno." She pointed to the bottle, pretending confusion. "But it was sort of harsh, so I dumped a bunch of sugar in it."

Seth snorted and leaned over for a look, gave a whistle. "Nice."

"Don brought it."

"He knows his wine."

"He knows his wine merchant." She got down a glass for Seth, sat by her half-finished one and released a shuddering sigh, giving in to the heavy peace that came after a good cry.

"So you dumped The Don, huh."

"I did." She stared miserably into her glass.

"Regrets?"

"No." She lifted her gaze to his. "None."

"Good." He reached over the table and took her hand. She let him. "Then it was the right move."

Bonnie nodded, looking down at their joined hands. His were so familiar. The freckle on the back of the right one; the scar where his younger brother had whacked him with a toy truck. He had other scars, too, on his body and on his heart. She knew all of them.

And suddenly she was finished fighting, finished struggling against what she felt for Seth. There would never be anyone else for her. The search on Seattledates had been about regaining personal power and self-esteem, not finding another man. She'd never wanted any other man. Not really.

Her gaze lifted to his again. She knew some of her vulnerability showed in her face, and she didn't try to hide it. No more games, no more hiding. If they were meant to be together, they would be. If not, she'd move out altogether, out of state. Maybe go to the other side of the country, like North Carolina or Maine, and start over. Buy a lighthouse and live there alone year-round, listening to the crash of the—

Good God, she'd go completely nuts. What was she thinking?

Pressure on her hand, then her arm. He was pulling her toward him, onto his lap.

Bonnie went, feeling as if she were going back home. She put her arm around his neck, rested her head against his. They sat that way a long time, Bonnie absorbing his strength, comfort and affection.

"Thank you, Seth." She lifted her head.

"For what?"

"Coming to my rescue, making me feel better."

"You're welcome, Bon." He smiled briefly, the goofy, wonderful smile that lit up his face so endearingly. "Remember, he's not the last man in the world."

"Thank God."

"You'll find someone. You're only just starting to look."

His words hurt, and she realized that subconsciously she'd been expecting him to try to get her back, the way he'd tried so many times in the past few months.

He'd learned. Finally. Good for him. Maybe he could really change. She hoped so. Because some lucky woman out there was going to get the finest man in the world.

"I'm thinking of leaving Seattle, maybe Washington." She couldn't believe she'd blurted out the words. She'd only just had the thought minutes ago. Why was she saying it out loud already?

And yet, as the words left her mouth, they became true

in a way she hadn't expected. Another victory for her sub-conscious.

"Bonnie." He stiffened in shock. "Why?"

"The shop isn't making it. And I need a change. I want to start over somewhere new."

He opened his mouth, closed it again. Stared at her for a long time, then gently pushed back bangs that had fallen into her eyes. His touch was gentle, tender and so sweet it made her heart ache.

"If that's what you want, then it's a good thing."

Her determination developed feet of panicky clay, and she straightened her spine. No, this wouldn't be the easiest decision, but maybe it was best.

"Thank you, Seth."

"I'd miss you. Like crazy."

"I'd miss you, too." The words came out easily, but they had a surreal quality, as if it weren't really possible for her and Seth to separate, as if somehow, sometime, a director would walk into the room and yell, "Okay, cut. Take five, everyone."

"Where are you thinking of going?"

"I don't know. Maine? My oldest brother went there for college. He loved it."

"Yeah," he said miserably. "But it's on the other side of the world."

"It is." She nodded, wishing for a few seconds that he'd beg her not to leave, insist he'd follow her anywhere, marry her, have kids, get a dog and live happily ever after.

But Seth wouldn't do that. Commitment wasn't his thing. And for her to stay sane, she needed to be as far away from him and what he would never give her as she could.

"One question. Promise you'll answer truthfully?"

"Sure." She lifted her head because she suddenly felt as

if she could never get enough of looking at his face, as if she hadn't already memorized every microinch of it.

"If the store was doing well, would you stay?"

"Seth." She gestured, then let her hand drop helplessly to her thighs. "The store *isn't* doing well. What is the point of—"

"You promised to answer the question."

She studied him for a few seconds, knowing the answer without having to think. Seattle was her home. "Yes."

"Okay. Thank you." He pulled her head down against his and closed his arms back around her once more, making her feel safe, protected and loved.

Bonnie closed her eyes, savoring every sensation as deeply as she could, knowing that in a few more weeks they could be saying goodbye forever.

11

"Ta daaa." Bonnie gestured to her computer. "Our new website. What do you think?"

Demi and the other Come to Your Senses residents peered at Bonnie's laptop in the common room. On the screen was a colorful, funky and appealing drawing of their building. On the sidebar, each business had a link over which was superimposed a cartoon of its owner, with features exaggerated to represent the five senses. Jack's face had large, dreamy eyes. Seth's head was turned in profile so his ears were front and center, Angela had gorgeous, plump lips, Demi was giving a flirty wave with both hands and Bonnie rapturously sniffed at some delicious fragrance. The overall effect was casual fun, colorful and very inviting.

"Bonnie, you did a *great* job." Angela put her hand on Bonnie's shoulder. "Really, that is amazing."

"Thanks." Bonnie's smile was brief. She'd been very subdued lately, had even been pleasant to Demi, which meant either she'd mellowed or had completely lost her mind. Demi couldn't claim to adore the woman, but she was worried about her. And given how the others treated her with kid gloves and traded anxious looks behind her back, they were worried, too.

"I love it," Demi said. "I think it sets just the right tone, perfect for the holiday special but also going forward after that."

"Agreed." Jack tipped his head to study it from another angle. "I like me with Bambi eyes."

"Yeah, real cute, Jack." Seth snorted. "Bonnie, you've outdone yourself."

Angela clapped her hands. "Good. Let's have beer to celebrate. I can go downstairs and get some cookies and a—"

"Not me." Bonnie glanced at her watch and hurriedly snapped her laptop closed. "I have to get going."

"Another date?" Demi asked.

"Sort of. Not really." She shoved back her chair, body tense. "More like a…business date."

Seth picked up her computer somberly. "I'll walk you."

"I'm out, too." Jack got up and stretched. "I'm meeting Melissa downstairs in five."

"Hot date?" Angela asked.

"Not really." His grin was unnaturally wide. "Just going to drive out to Seward Park."

Angela wrinkled her brow. "Didn't you guys do a photo shoot there?"

"Uh-huh." Still grinning. Possibly even wider.

"What about you, Demi?" Angela turned to her. "Want to share a beer? Or a six-pack?"

Demi hesitated, squashing the shy demons that said Angela had asked her just to be polite after the rest of her *real* friends couldn't make it.

Then just as quickly she told herself not to react like that anymore. Positive thinking! About time she followed her own advice. She wasn't meeting Colin for another hour and a half. She had plenty of time for a beer.

"I can't stay long, but I'd love to."

"Got a date?" Jack stood swinging his arms back and

forth. He was definitely on edge tonight. Was something going around?

"I'm going to the Earshot Jazz Festival."

"You're going with Colin." He wasn't asking.

She stared at him curiously. "How did you know?"

"You look like someone is lighting firecrackers inside you."

"Yeah?" Demi pointed accusingly. "Well, so do you."

"I rest my case." He left the room, chuckling.

Demi made a growling noise in her throat and turned to Angela. "How can you stand living with these caring, warm and supportive people?"

Angela burst into giggles on her way to the refrigerator. "I know, I know, it's painful. Jack was antsy as hell tonight, though, wasn't he?"

"Another of his photography shows opening?"

"Don't think so. But he's been doing really well after that big one of Melissa at the Unko Gallery." Angela rummaged in the refrigerator. "Hey, there's some good cheese in here, too. Help me find crackers. We'll have a party."

Demi crossed to the cabinets and began searching. "Here's a crazy idea. Think he's going to ask Melissa to marry him tonight?"

"Oh, my God!" Angela straightened, gasping. "They're going to Seward Park. I bet you're right!"

"Just a guess."

"No, no, I know, we could be totally wrong. But I hope we're not." She laid out the cheese on a plate and added a knife. "I'm not going to be able to stand the suspense!"

"Me neither." Demi brought down a box of crackers and a plate, and started arranging, enjoying hanging out with Angela. She should ask her to lunch sometime, or dinner, or maybe to a chick flick. "How are things with you and Daniel?"

"Blissful. Stupidly, hopelessly, ridiculously blissful. I know it's the worst cliché on the planet, but I'm going to say it anyway. I did not know it could be like this."

"Oh, gosh. That's wonderful, Angela." Demi beamed at her, then resumed her cabinet search and found some pretzels and a jar of mixed nuts to add to the party, thinking of the night she'd spent with Colin, all the overwhelming and exhilarating and terrifying emotions that had buffeted her around endlessly. "Can I ask a dumb relationship question?"

"Well, of course. All dumb questions encouraged. Besides, there's nothing I like better than talking about Daniel, and the other three are sick to death of hearing about how perfect he is."

"How did you know that what you were feeling wasn't just infatuation or lust?" She held her breath, waiting for teasing, but Angela simply passed her a beer, looking thoughtful.

"That's a tough one. Because once you've been around, you know that initial thrill can happen with people who aren't right for you same as those who are. But with Daniel...it was just more. More feeling, more excitement, more fireworks, but also more trust, more contentment, a more conscious awareness that our values and lives and habits meshed really well.

"And I like who I am around him. He doesn't change me, but I've dated other men who did—hell, I *married* one. Around my ex I was a horrible, insecure mess. I'm nothing like that with Daniel. We bring out good things in each other." She opened her own beer. "See? I'll talk about him all day if you let me."

"It's fine. Actually that was perfect. I just feel with Colin..." She followed Angela back into the common room, and set the snacks and beer on the coffee table, then sat on the couch, trying to frame her jumble of feelings into words that might make sense, ridiculously happy that she had someone kind and caring and female who'd listen. "I feel as if it's too soon to be feeling this much, and I can't trust it. As if it's so different that it can't be real, because I can't control it or label it or… I mean, it's like I'm going around and around, beating myself up over— *What* is so funny?"

Angela had her hand over her mouth to keep from spraying beer. "If Bonnie was here she'd die. I was saying exactly the same stuff about Daniel months ago. Seriously, if I had a transcript I think it was word for word. Or close."

"Argh." Demi smacked a hand to her forehead. "But I don't *like* this. It doesn't make sense that someone like him would want someone like me."

Angela's left eyebrow rose. "You mean a beautiful, funny, talented woman?"

"You should have seen his last girlfriend."

"Who he's not seeing anymore."

"Because she dumped him." She started counting on her fingers. "I'm shy, he's not. I'm a homebody, he likes going out. He's rebounding, he's a mess because of his injury, he's—"

"Oh, way to focus on the positives." Angela brought out her counting fingers, too. "How about he likes you, he wants to be with you and you guys are checking each other out to see if there's a fit? It's called dating."

Was it really that simple?

"When we started, it did seem that easy, but…" Her body slumped against the couch cushions. "I don't want to get hurt."

"Aw, sweetie." Angela's face turned gentle. "No, you don't. At the same time, if you want to find out what can happen between you, you can't hold back, either, because then you're cheating each other out of who you really are and you won't get a true picture."

Demi groaned, attacking cheese with the knife. "I liked it better when I thought he was a jerk."

"I know, I know. Dating sucks. And I know you're thinking easy for me to say, I'm happy. But I wasn't for a long time. I know how scary it is. For years after my divorce I didn't date anyone. I thought I was being strong. Nuh-uh. Just chicken. At least you're trying."

Demi passed her cheese on a cracker. "What made you want to date again?"

Angela shrugged, taking on that beaming, melty expression Demi had seen her and Jack wearing multiple times when they were talking about their beloveds. "Daniel walked into my shop. Knocked me for a loop."

Oh, boy. Demi knew what that felt like. Colin had walked into her waiting room. "You think it was love at first sight?"

"Oh, no, just big old lust. Love came later." She grinned. "By the way, I'm so glad you're hanging around with us more, Demi. It's really great. We felt sort of awkward for a while, like you didn't enjoy our company."

Demi's jaw dropped. "You're kidding. I avoided everyone because you were such good friends I thought I'd be intruding."

"No, not at all. I think you're fabulous. Seth and Jack, too. And Bonnie…"

"Yeah, I know. Bonnie hates me."

"Bonnie makes snap judgments. She'll get over it once she spends more time with you." Angela's pretty brows drew down. "I'm worried about her. Something's going on, and I can't get her to talk about it. We've always been close but this is really worrying me. I'm terrified she's sick or something. She's lost so much weight."

Demi shook her head. "She doesn't seem sick to me. Just sad and worried."

"Definitely sad. I wonder if— Oh, geez." Angela jumped, then hauled her phone out of her pocket. Her face lit like the sun.

"Say hi to Daniel." Demi stood up, giggling.

Angela looked startled. "How did you know it was him?"

"Easy." She took one more cheese slice for the road. "Your internal firecrackers."

"Ha! The damn things won't stop when he's around. Have fun on your date!" She gave a brief wave, and answered the phone with a "hi" so blissful Demi couldn't decide whether to giggle or be envious. So she did both.

Back in her apartment, she thought about those firecrackers while getting dressed in black pants paired with a red sweater, and her favorite dangling earrings given to her by her mom for her twenty-first birthday—gold thread twisted around red coral beads. Thought about them as she painted her lips a matching red, squirted on the faintest spray of eau de cologne her sister gave her years ago, which she'd worn maybe three times, and went downstairs to wait, even though it was early.

Everything Angela had said about falling in love with Daniel described how Demi felt about Colin. From the fireworks, to the sense of newness, to the better person she was around him. The way she was conquering her shyness, the way she was free to indulge her sensuality.

Only problem? She didn't want to fall in love with Colin. Because he was only just beginning the process of figuring out who postaccident Colin would be. And because deep down she didn't believe he could truly fall in love with her.

So the best thing she could do, the most sensible, anyway, would be to acknowledge she was developing feelings for him and say, *So what? Que sera, sera.* She'd ride this boat until it got her where she wanted to go or capsized and she drowned.

Her phone rang and she fumbled for it, then rolled her eyes. Carrie. Demi had never returned her last call. She'd better pick up. "Hi, Carrie."

"Hey, little sister. What are you doing?" Her voice cracked; she sounded weirdly manic.

"I'm about to go to a jazz concert." For once she had something exciting to report. "How about you?"

"Oh, that sounds fun. Who's playing?"

"Full Nelson."

"I love them! You lucky. Who are you going with?"

"A guy I'm dating. Colin Russo."

Her sister's scream of excitement made Demi jerk the phone away from her ear. Was there a polite way to tell someone to dial herself down? "Demi, how great! I'm so glad you took my advice."

Her advice? "Thanks."

Carrie sighed dramatically. "I so envy you. Always have."

"Uh." Did Demi hear that correctly? "Did you say you envy me?"

"Your life is still evolving. I mean, you still have so much ahead of you. I settled down so early, and…I don't know. I feel sort of stuck sometimes. Like I'm running in these meaningless circles and not really getting anywhere."

Her sister's speech sounded a little sloppy, and Demi suspected she'd been drinking. This was a totally unexpected side of Perfect Carrie. "You've always made it sound as if you had the ideal life."

"I've been in therapy. I'm working a lot of stuff out. I'm not sure I married the right man, Demi." She started crying. "I'm not sure I'm living the right life for me. I've been trying to be Mom and I'm not Mom. Trying to be someone you're not is a horrible mistake."

"Carrie, honey. Listen, I'm about to get picked up. Why

don't we go out sometime so we can really talk?" She stood on the steps, feeling totally disoriented. Did she really just voluntarily suggest she and her sister spend time together?

"I would love that." Carrie sniffed several times. "I feel like I'm the only loser in the family. Mike is perfect, you're perfect."

"Perfect?" Demi's voice squeaked. "Me? Are you kidding? I'm the alien child. Don't like people. Can't handle parties. Haven't gotten married…"

"None of those are bad things, they're just different."

"Yeah, I'm different all right. You and Mom were in total sync."

"I was copying her," Carrie said glumly. "I have no personality of my own. No talents that matter in the world."

"That's not true." Demi could not take all of this in. How could she not have had any idea how much pain her sister was in? Was everyone in her family this good at hiding their real selves? They should all have been spies. "For one thing, you can make cakes that look like hats, and for another, you can virtual shop for jewelry with the best of them."

Her sister giggled. "That I can do."

Inspiration hit: Edwin's Jewelers. "I know. Come downtown Monday, Carrie, after work. I have this great necklace we can both buy."

"Expensive?"

"Through the roof."

"Diamonds?"

"Dozens."

"I'm there." She giggled again, still sniffling. "Thanks, Demi. You're the best."

Demi hung up the phone, still feeling as if she'd been transported to an alternate universe. Her perfect sister with the perfect life was a mess.

Maybe that was something she needed to keep in mind

when she found herself trying too hard to make her own life about order and logic, and kept beating herself up for simply being human.

Ya think, Demi?

"Want a ride, gorgeous?"

She started, then stood still while, yes, the firecrackers, predictable by now, went nuts inside her. How long had Colin been there?

"Yes, please." She ran down the steps and into his car, grinning at him, feeling freer and happier than she had in a while. Relieved of the burden of judging herself so harshly? Or of feeling harshly judged by others—her sister, the Come to Your Senses bunch. Most likely it was all part of the same thing. "Hello."

"Hi." He leaned over for a brief kiss and pulled out into traffic, then turned left onto Broadway. "You look absolutely gorgeous."

"So do you." She was not remotely exaggerating. He was smoking hot dressed in a black shirt and black pants. "How is your back? I'm asking of course as a concerned friend, not a physical therapist."

"No, of course not. I took a quick run yesterday, a slow half mile, and it was fine. I'm going to build up from nothing if it kills me."

"Oh, don't let it do that."

"I won't." He took her hand, gave it a squeeze. "And neither will your friend Julie, who is not nearly as talented as you, but she's helping."

"Julie is a doll." She sat back, smile permaglued to her lips, feeling positively bubbly. "What else is going on?"

"I'm going back to work next week at the health club. Been practicing my sax. I've started making you a knife."

She touched the back of her hand to his cheek. "Life feeling good these days?"

He pulled up to a red light. "Yeah, Demi. Life is feeling really good."

Joy swamped her. She was practically in tears. "That is fantastic."

"You're responsible, you know." He turned those devastating eyes on her, which made it even harder not to cry.

"Nah." Her voice was shaky. "I might have given you a shove, but you would have found your way back without me."

"It was a good shove."

She beamed at him until the car behind them politely honked that the light had turned green. "Speaking of shoves, was giving me these tickets a little hint that I needed to get out more?"

"Maybe. But I was hoping you'd ask me to go with you."

"Oh, so I fell right in with your diabolical plan?"

He cackled evilly. "You did, yes."

"The same way I fell into having lunch with you, and coming over when you were hurt, and staying the night and—"

"Face it, you have no hope of resisting me." He turned onto Madison. "None."

Demi laughed to cover the fear that he was right. "I better stop trying?"

"I'm telling you, resistance is futile."

"Okay, then." Demi glanced at him again, unable to stop looking. How she was going to bear sitting next to him for three hours, keeping her hands to herself, she had no idea. He'd turned her into a junkie for his body, for his scent, for the way he felt and the way he made her feel.

"Who were you talking to when I pulled up? You looked shell-shocked."

"My sister. She was acting…not like herself. Usually our conversations consist of her making sure I know how much more rewarding and impressive and enjoyable her life is than mine, plus loads of advice on how I could become more like her."

"Not a happy person, huh." He glanced over to get her reaction. "Jealous of you maybe?"

"What— How did you—" She laughed, shaking her head. "Was I the only person who couldn't see that?"

"I'm sure she fooled lots of people." He shrugged. "It's easier to see when it's not your baggage."

"Maybe it's true of your family, too? Your overachiever brothers?"

"Yes, but no. None of them wants to be a half-crippled personal trainer." He flashed her a grin. "Sorry, was I pouting again? I accepted a long time ago that I love my family, but I don't always like them. And I don't need them to like me. It's helped."

Demi nodded. "I think we share that attitude."

"And a lot of others if you've noticed." He turned right on Eighth Avenue and passed Town Hall to park at the garage a few blocks farther north. "Ready?"

"Sure." She climbed out of his car and took his hand, nearly toppling off her heels when he swung her around and dragged her up against him, then kissed her until she could barely think straight.

"Sorry." He released her and gently brushed hair off her forehead. "There was just no way I could make it to intermission without that."

"I'm completely fine with it." Her voice was breathless, giddy. "Anytime, really. Love to help."

He grinned, kissed her again, then drew back. "I like you, Demi."

Oh, my. The phrase went into her ears and triggered in her brain an astonishing array of pleasure sensations. "I like you, too, Colin."

They smiled at each other until it felt horribly awkward, then they laughed at themselves and their goofy infatuation, held hands and flew to the Town Hall.

Flew. Seriously. Demi had never understood the concept of feet not touching the ground, but she wasn't aware of any contact between sole and cement. Ah, the joys of being with this man all in black whose kisses erased her brain.

The Great Hall was packed for the concert. She and Colin had excellent spots on the wooden benches, aisle seats in the front section only a few rows back. This place was one of her favorite concert venues. Not only did it have excellent acoustics, but with its stained-glass windows, vaulting and central dome, it felt like an ancient church more suited to Europe than the States.

Today, however, she barely blinked at her surroundings. Something much more magnetic and compelling was sitting right next to her, not cool stone or dark wood, but hot flesh and pulsing blood.

Oh, my goodness. She had it bad tonight. Lust? Infatuation? More?

Oops. She'd promised herself not to wonder. Just to enjoy.

Full Nelson entered in all its long-haired, tattooed glory, and started to play. Demi knew they were good, but her brain would not pay attention. She could only sit there, experiencing Colin's thigh pressed against the length of hers, the way their hips met, the perfect way her shoulder fit against the side of his chest, the way she wanted to touch and taste every part of him.

This was not a good night for a concert. This was a good night for opening a bottle of wine, building a fire and making love in front of it. For hours.

Oooh, Colin had a fireplace at his condo...

Her thoughts became happily occupied with that scenario. The music drifted past her hearing as she focused on herself and Colin in his condo, wine in their glasses, Colin lighting a blaze, turning out lights, standing tall and proud, slowly stripping off his…everything.

Shirt first, unbuttoning black cotton, widening the V that let his golden skin show, until he slipped it off his shoulders, so muscled and masculine. In her mind the shirt floated to the floor like a leaf in autumn, and his hands moved in an equally leisurely manner to the fly of his black pants, unsnapping, unzipping, showing black material underneath, boxer briefs that clung to his trim hips and powerful thighs.

Down went the pants, unwrapping more golden skin beneath hair that glinted in the light.

Then his briefs went down and down, revealing the perfection of his build, head to toe, the magnificent cock springing free. In her imagination she was drawn over to him, naked herself. She put her hands to his hard shoulders, slid them over his curving solid pecs, let them ski moguls over his abdominals. She knelt and took him into her mouth, feeling the warmth of the firelight at her back, seeing it dance in his eyes when she looked up and—

The audience burst into applause, making her body jerk with panic.

"Whoa." Colin smirked at her. "Did you drift off there?"

"No, no, of course not." She clapped maniacally hard. "That was great, wasn't it?"

"Uh-huh. What was that number at the end of the set?"

"Oh, it was…" She pretended to think. "Hmm, I can't remember the name of it."

His eyebrows rose. "Variations on a little tune called 'Twinkle, Twinkle Little Star.'"

Oops. She wrinkled her nose. "Um, okay, you got me. I was kind of thinking about something else."

"Yeah?" He was clearly more amused than offended as

he put his arm around her and hugged her close. "What were you thinking about?"

"Well…" She leaned up for a lingering kiss and drew her hand down his chest. "You and me. Totally naked. Making love in front of a fire—"

"Excuse me?"

Colin and Demi turned to find a rowful of people waiting to get out for intermission.

"Sorry." Colin jumped up and took Demi's hand, leading her into the aisle. He grabbed his coat and then hers.

"Ready to go?"

"It's just intermission." She gestured to the stage. "The second half…"

"I know." He winked. "Ready to go?"

Her smile grew wicked. "Go where, Colin?"

"My place."

"Fireplace?"

"Yes, ma'am." He practically dragged her down the aisle. "I'm going to drive like you, so we'll be there in about three minutes. Then I want you to show me exactly what you were thinking about."

12

COLIN DIDN'T QUITE get them home from Town Hall in three minutes, but it wasn't a whole lot longer. He loved jazz. He loved Full Nelson. But he'd barely heard a note of the concert. The entire time he'd been aware of Demi sitting beside him, how she breathed, how she moved, how her body felt against him. So when she'd stopped moving, and her eyes had glazed over, he'd realized she wasn't listening to the music any more than he was.

Someday the two of them would be able to get through a concert, but not yet, not when the desire for each other was still so strong.

Someday? When had he started thinking longer-term with Demi? She'd been receptive to his lovemaking, but emotionally neither of them had taken any risks. Maybe tonight he would. Because clearly his feelings for her went beyond the physical. Since meeting her he'd gotten back in touch with someone other than the one-track jock he'd become, unaware of the narrowness of his own life. Stephanie had done nothing to broaden it, and when he'd needed her most, she'd deserted him. With Demi he was discovering how honest intimacy could enrich his life—and him.

For the first time he wondered what he could bring to

her life, and immediately promised himself to make sure there was plenty. He hadn't ever worried about that with Stephanie. Apparently he'd figured the gift of his manliness was enough.

Demi was making him more humble, too.

She was amazing.

He parked the car and took her hand on the way up to his apartment. He was going to take this slowly. He wanted to make love to her in front of his fireplace, just the way she'd been daydreaming about during the concert. He would make the experience between them so erotic, so emotionally charged, that it would be impossible for her not to realize how good they were together and commit to finding out if she could have serious feelings for him. Because he was pretty sure, even in this incredibly short time, that he was damn serious about her.

The thought was so overwhelming, so emotional, that he could only stand there, clutching her hand, watching the floors count higher, feeling like there was a warm honey-covered balloon gradually inflating in his chest. Beside him Demi was also quiet, poised as always, but he could sense her anticipation was as high as his. He could only hope it was for the same reason.

Inside his apartment, he took off his jacket, helped her off with hers, then slid his hand down her cheek. She was so beautiful, so hot tonight, the lady in red. He didn't think Demi had noticed, but she'd caught many men's eyes on the street and in Town Hall tonight, which had made half of him want to strut with she's-with-me pride, and the other half growl with my-woman possessiveness.

Now he had her alone and he was going to make her fantasy come true.

"Tell me what you want, Demi," he whispered. "What were you thinking about during the show?"

Her shy smile made his heart beat almost painfully. Her hands landed on his chest and slid up around his neck. "You *really* want to know?"

"Uh...yeah?"

He loved her easy laugh. "Okay, we were drinking wine here in your apartment."

"Which room?"

"Living. Don't interrupt."

"Sorry, I have to." He kissed her, drawing her close, savoring her soft lips clinging to his. They were good together. She had to realize that. "Okay, interruption over, keep going."

"Well." She was laughing now. "I guess *that* kind of interruption is okay."

"Better than. Go on."

"Okay. The fire was lit, and you were standing by it." Her voice was slow and dreamy. He was getting hard already and they hadn't done anything. "You took your clothes off, piece by piece. I couldn't take my eyes off your body in the firelight."

"Mmm, I like this fantasy a lot."

"Inter-rupting," she sang.

He snorted, nearly drunk with how crazy he was about her. "Sorry, go on."

"I was already naked, by the way."

"You—mmph." Her hand landed on his mouth, so he pulled her hips tight against him instead. Who needed words? The way her eyes widened, then narrowed with pleasure made him even harder.

"So then..." She started circling her pelvis against him, making him groan beneath her fingers. "I went over to you and knelt down in front of you and took your beautiful, hard cock deep in my mouth."

His eyes crossed. She giggled and took her hand away, started to pull back. "You are terrible," she accused.

"You are killing me." He pulled her back against him just this side of roughly. "And you are remarkable. You even give to me in the privacy of your mind, where you can have anything you want happen."

"Yeah." She pushed away again and pulled her sweater up and over her head. "I'm pretty much a saint."

His jaw fell open. No saint. Seriously sexy sinner. Under the sweater Demi had on a lacy red bra that pushed her breasts up into paradise. "Oh, my—"

"C'mon, baby." She posed, her fabulous breasts thrust forward, one leg pointed slightly out. "Light my fire."

"Duh." He pretended stupor. "Soon as my brain reboots."

"Oh, wine, too." She moved her hips in a slow circle. "We need wine."

"Mmmm." He took her shoulders, tasted the soft skin of her neck, bent down to press his face to the beautiful rounds of her breasts. Demi dropped her head back, let him explore.

Oh, what this woman did to him. And what he wanted to do to her...

Somehow he tore his mouth from her skin. "Wine. Fire. Let's do this."

He managed to walk into the kitchen and open the refrigerator. No white in there. He opened the cabinet where he kept his reds.

When he had any.

"Uh. Demi, I'm out of... Does beer work?"

"Beer?" She shoved hands on her hips, pretending disgust. "That's the best you can do?"

"Brandy?"

She looked pained, her brown eyes dancing. "I *guess* that would work."

"Whew." He got down snifters and poured, then led her over to the fireplace. "Epic fail on the wine. But we do have the fire. This will still work. You ready?"

"Oh, yes." She looked like a men's magazine centerfold, red lips matching her bra, her dark hair and pink cheeks contrasting perfectly with the pale cream of her skin. Yes, he'd be very happy to have her kneeling in front of him— what guy wouldn't?—but he really wanted to make love to her. And as soon as her fantasy played out, he'd take her into his bedroom and make sure he showed her exactly how important she was becoming to him.

"Behold. I give you fire." He grinned cockily and flicked the switch. Nothing happened. He flicked the switch off, then on again.

Nothing. Off again. On again. He started to sweat.

Damn it. He hated to disappoint her. Again.

But she was giggling. "Wow, this is *just* like my fantasy."

"Demi, I swear, this has never happened." He flicked the switch again in desperation. If at first you totally screw up… "It's always worked fine."

"I guess you just can't get hot for me, Colin."

"You have no idea."

"Fine." She sighed. "I can see I'm going to have to take over myself if I want to get anything done here."

He flicked the switch one more ridiculously hopeful time, then crouched and peered under the pseudo-logs. Was the pilot light out? Was there some kind of blockage under there? He poked around, trying to see if…

Some instinct told him it would be a very good idea to turn around.

He did.

It was.

While he'd been ineptly staring into his fireplace, Demi had been very ably removing her clothes. She was smiling Mona-Lisa-like, holding her glass, siren-stunning, but also—and this pleased him even more—completely comfortable standing naked in his living room. No shyness, no blushes.

He wanted her here often. She could even have an article or two of clothing on sometimes. Once in a while. Maybe.

"Ungh."

"Sorry?" She sauntered toward him. "Didn't quite catch that?"

"Naked. Woman. Naked."

"Man. Clothed." She pursed her lips in disapproval.

His clothes came off faster than they ever had. Also naked, he stood by the not-fire across from his gorgeous siren, thinking he'd never had so much fun with a girlfriend in his life. Sex with other women had been so earnest and he'd always felt pressure to make it movie-perfect.

"Very nice." She sipped her brandy through those fabulous red lips, eyes enormous in her face. She looked happy. And hot as hell.

"Demi, I know I didn't get the fantasy *quite* perfect, but maybe we can salvage it a little?"

She put her glass down and stood close enough that he could feel the heat from her body and smell her light perfume and her own enticing Demi-fragrance. His cock rose.

"I think we can manage just fine." Her hands landed on his shoulders; she kissed a trail down his stomach, then knelt gracefully and took him into her mouth.

"Oh, Demi." He groaned, closed his eyes, felt her warm tongue on him, her fingers gently fondling his balls. His knees nearly gave out; he shifted and reached out to touch her—

Pain shot through his back; his body jerked uncontrollably and Demi's teeth…

Ow!

"I'm so sorry." She took hold of his rapidly shrinking penis, examining it tenderly. "I *bit* you, my God. I'm so, *so* sorry."

"It's fine. I'm fine." He was. But her fantasy was now officially toast, and he felt worse about that than being bitten.

"Was it your back?" She stood, clearly stricken. "Are you okay?"

"Yes." He gave her a reassuring smile. "Just a quick shot of pain. And teeth marks are the very coolest thing on penises now."

"I feel so bad I—" She must have heard his comment in delay mode, because she suddenly burst out laughing so hard it made him laugh, too. And nothing in the world felt better than sharing a belly laugh with Demi.

Well, maybe one thing. But she might have had enough of that for one evening.

"Oh, my gosh." She giggled a few more times, wiping her eyes. "Can we give up on the fantasy? I think we should just go into the bedroom."

"Maybe it's safer." He pulled her close and kissed her, intending a quick lighthearted peck, but she felt so soft and so right and so...*naked* that he couldn't stop.

"Make love to me, Colin," she whispered.

Who was he to say no to a naked siren he was falling for? In his room they climbed onto the bed and moved toward each other without ceremony, without trappings, man and woman together, natural and right.

When he entered her, her eyes stayed open. It seemed natural to gaze at each other, sharing the wonder of what their bodies were feeling. And sharing something deeper that Colin had suspected was there all along.

He moved slowly, wanting their lovemaking to go on all night, all weekend, all month, maybe forever. She was hot and tight around him, fit him perfectly. She gave herself completely, wide-open to him, letting him know with her hands, her hips, her breaths, moans and whispered words how much he was pleasing her.

Every thrust, every caress, she was right there with him. He'd never felt so connected to another human being. This was what sex was supposed to be like. This was what poets and playwrights went into raptures over, what men killed for.

Not just sex. Making love. He'd never felt such depth of feeling for any other woman before this, and it both scared and thrilled him.

Because there was only one conclusion to be drawn from this experience, from these feelings and from the thoughts he'd started having about a future with Demi in it.

He loved her.

"YOU'RE WELCOME. ENJOY them." Bonnie waved the woman out of her shop and slumped onto the stool behind her counter. Good lord, were pigs flying out there? Should she order up some ice from hell? Bonnie Blooms had been overrun with customers and phone orders that morning—a Sunday. Outside it was dismal, rainy and cold. Usually people stayed home in droves in bad weather, except for special occasions, though some people needed the bright color and scent of flowers to perk them up in grim weather. Maybe that's what was happening today? Bonnie Blooms had been here nearly two years and she'd never had such good business.

The irony of course was that the upturn was happening just as she'd decided to give up on the store, though she couldn't count on the rush continuing. Bonnie didn't need to make bucketloads of money, that was never her goal. She'd just wanted desperately to stay in business. To take her crazy dream and make it work.

But given how badly she was in debt, it would take more than a few days of above-average business to get her out of danger and make her change her mind. She would need the foot traffic to continue, plus several standing orders from companies.

She gazed around her shop, thinking of all the hopes that had gone into it, all the work and the pride.

Might as well admit that for all her excitement over the vague notion of starting over somewhere else, it would rip her heart out to leave this behind.

Another customer walked in. Looked like a college kid, earphone wires hanging from his ears.

"Hey." He grinned at her, bobbing his head up and down like a seal to some beat only he could hear. "How's it going?"

"Fine." She wasn't sure what was wrong with him but obviously something was. He was probably high—Bonnie hoped he wouldn't be violent or otherwise unruly. The last thing she needed after a day like today was someone robbing the register.

"It's really you." He took out his earbuds and pointed at her, advancing slowly. Bonnie gripped the counter, wondering when to start screaming. "From YouTube."

From YouTube? She was from Seattle. "Sorry, you must have me mixed up with—"

"No, no, no." He was still grinning that weird squinty-eyed grin. "It's you. Bonnie from Bonnie Blooms, right?"

"Yeah…" She wanted him to leave. Now. He was creeping her out.

"Your video. About your store. It's really cool. I love that guy. He rocks."

She stared blankly. The kid was out of his mind. How was she going to—

"C'mon. You know who I'm talking about. Seth something."

Bonnie started. "Seth Blackstone?"

"Yeah, yeah, that's the guy. He posts those great songs to YouTube."

"I've heard them."

"There's the one about you."

She blinked at him. "About me."

"Hang on." He pulled an iPhone out of his pocket and tapped the keypad, gazed at the screen earnestly for a minute, then shoved the device into her hands. "There."

Bonnie took it reluctantly and watched the clip stream by, curious at first, then stunned and then very emotional. Suddenly the whole morning made sense. And now that she thought back, a couple of people had mentioned seeing a video. But she'd been frantically busy filling multiple orders—something she wasn't used to doing—and hadn't really paid attention, just nodded politely and moved on to the next customer.

Seth had written a song. A silly, fun, catchy song about a shop on Capitol Hill. How the owner was a lady with special powers to bring joy, comfort and love into the lives of the people who bought her flowers. The video was scattered with clips of her, which he must have gotten over the years and from her parents, interspersed with close-ups of stills. In one clip from her childhood she was dressed as a fairy princess carrying a magic wand. In another she was proudly gesturing to the garden she'd designed in her parents' backyard. Later came pictures of her laughing with employees of Blossoms Dearie and dancing at a Halloween party hosted by Come to Your Senses, dressed as a daisy; and finally, during the closing refrain, a lingering close-up of the picture Jack had taken of Bonnie wearing nothing but flowers. Probably her favorite picture of all time.

Life would be tragic without her sweet magic
My bonnie Bonnie Blooms only for me.

Tears filled her eyes. *Oh, Seth.*

She sniffled and handed the iPhone back to the kid. "Thank you for showing me this."

"Sure." He looked aimlessly around the shop. "Hey, so, can I have some flowers? My girlfriend loves this stuff."

"Absolutely." She could barely concentrate on what he was saying. "How much did you want to spend?"

"Aw, I dunno. Fifteen?"

"Coming right up." She wrapped up an appropriate bouquet on autopilot, though did think to put in a few extra blooms to thank him, and signed a grubby piece of paper he provided for her autograph. Her autograph!

As soon as he left, she rushed to the phone to call Seth…

But more customers came in. And then more phone calls. Apparently his latest upload was also a hit. Apparently people wanted to check her out.

By the end of the day, she'd had fifty-three walk-ins and forty-two phone orders, about triple her busiest day so far. But it didn't stop there. She had a call from a hotel, another from an exclusive downtown women's clothing boutique. Both were looking for a florist for regular deliveries, would she be able to show them what she could do?

It took every ounce of Bonnie's self-control not to shout, "Yes! Please! You have no idea!"

By the time she closed up her store, she was absolutely exhausted and absolutely exhilarated.

And she had someone to thank.

She checked her stock, updated her financial records, wrote out a new order for the wholesale shop and locked up. Instead of rushing upstairs, though, she went out onto Broadway to the specialty grocery store she generally avoided, opting instead to drive to the big bargain super-market some miles away.

Not tonight.

She bought mixed roasted nuts, cheese, champagne recommended by the guy in the wine department, French bread, raspberries, paper-thin slices of prosciutto, a mixed green salad with walnuts and red onion, and one of the gorgeous glazed fruit tarts she'd coveted in the window for months and effing months.

Now it was all going to be hers. And Seth's.

On her way back to the Come to Your Senses building—her home!—she dug out her cell and dialed him. "Hey, Seth, it's me."

"Hi, me."

"You doing anything right now?"

"Just finishing a song."

She grinned. She'd get to hear it when it was finished. This one and all the others he wrote from now on. Maybe they'd end up together, maybe not. Maybe she'd find some-one else, maybe not. But Maine could stay right where it was, and she'd go visit when she managed to have a little extra change. She hadn't come this far to give up. Not on Bonnie Blooms. Not on Seth. He hadn't given up on her.

"Feel like having some dinner? My treat."

"Bonnie, I'm happy to buy you—"

"No, no. My treat. Ramen noodles and kidney beans. Can I come up?"

"Always, Bonnie."

She took a moment to close her eyes blissfully, then sprinted up the front steps, charged down the hall and up the staircase, too impatient to wait for the elevator. In front of his door, she put down the grocery bags and no, she didn't knock, she *hammered*.

"Okay, okay." Seth opened the door, looking bleary-eyed and tousled as he always did when he was composing. "What's the—"

She didn't give him the chance to finish, just jumped into his arms and kissed him with everything she had.

The second she finished and pulled away to thank him, he grabbed her back and kissed her with everything *he* had. Which was plenty.

"Okay, now tell me." He loosened his grip, as breathless as she was. "Dinner, kissing…what's the occasion?"

"You did the video! People were coming and calling in all day, and Razia's Dress Boutique and the Greymont Hotel want to see if I can fill regular orders. And it's all because you—"

He kissed her with such relief and passion that she thought she was going to have to scream to let her joy out.

"I had no idea what would happen, so I didn't say anything. I couldn't bear to get your hopes up in case the video tanked."

"It didn't." She laughed from sheer excitement. "All day long I was either making sales or answering the—"

"Does this mean you're not leaving?"

"Hell yes."

He gave a shout and swung her around, kissed her again and again until she considered pleading for mercy. "I didn't see how you could."

"I don't think I really ever was going to. It always seemed a little unreal. I needed an escape hatch, I guess. But the store is everything to me."

He grew still. "Everything, Bonnie?"

"Not quite." She smiled tenderly, messing his messy hair further. "Seth, you are definitely…something to me."

He laughed. "I'll take that for now."

"Oh, I left dinner outside."

"The ramen and beans? Uh, about that. I have some steaks I can thaw in the microwave."

"No, no, this is my treat." She darted to the hall and lugged in their dinner.

"Really, Bon, it wouldn't take me any time and I can whip up a…" His eyes bulged at the sight of the bags. "Holy crap, that is a *lot* of beans and ramen noodles."

"I know." She marched into his kitchen and started unloading, hearing his chuckles behind her. "I splurged just a little."

"I'll say you did."

"You deserve it." She turned and patted his cheek.

He grabbed her hand, held it to his face, then kissed it, slowly, each finger, then her palm, letting his tongue linger on her skin.

Fire started low in her belly, traveled down between her legs. Oh, this man…

He lowered her hand, looking about as serious and sincere as she'd ever seen him. Her heart started beating way too fast. A choice was coming. One that would determine what happened between them for the next few hours, and maybe the next…who knew? With Seth it was always impossible to tell.

"I want to play you this song I wrote."

Bonnie swallowed, disappointed. Maybe *she'd* have to offer the choice, since she was the one who'd walked away this time. "Sure. I'd love to hear it."

She followed him into his studio, thinking fondly of how much time she'd spent up here with him, trying out songs, giving him advice, making him laugh. And that one special time a few months ago, tearing up the room with wildly hot sex.

He took his guitar out of its case, pulled his stool close

to the chair she always sat in and tuned his instrument with unusual concentration, frown between his brows.

He was nervous.

Last time he'd been nervous playing her a song, it had been about falling in love, unusual for him. His songs were all about heartbreak, cheating and doubt.

She'd wondered at the time if that song had been a message to her.

Seth strummed a few chords, readjusted his position. "Okay."

"Okay." She was nervous, too, and she wasn't even sure why. But the powerful sensation was back, telling her the choice would be hers to make—here, and very, very soon.

He started to play a simple arpeggiated line then began to sing. "Roses are red. Violets are blue. I wanted to tell you that I love you."

"Seriously?" She screwed up her face in distaste. He didn't hit every time, but he'd never composed a clunker like this before.

"Shh." He strummed a few more times. "Don't interrupt. There's more."

"Gee, I can hardly wait."

"Violets are blue, roses are red. This song is to ask if you want to be wed."

"Seth. Stop, it's awful. What were you thinking?"

"Bonnie you bloom here in my heart. I cannot bear us to be apart. You're part of me, all warm inside. And I'm asking you to be my bride. You make me laugh, you make me smile, please walk with me down the aisle."

The last chord faded away. He lowered his instrument. "What do you think?"

She was staring, frozen, unable to dare hope.

"Okay, I know it stunk. Let me try again." He took the guitar off his neck, slid from the stool and knelt at her feet, looking up with such vulnerability that she almost couldn't connect him with the man she knew, almost couldn't bear to look.

And yet. It was Seth. On his knees. And if she wasn't mistaken...

"I'm asking you to be with me for the rest of my life, Bonnie. To belong to me the way I belong to you, and have for years, only I was too stupid and scared to be able to handle it. I've been working like a dog in therapy so I could deserve you, so I could feel whole enough to ask for what I've wanted all my life."

Tears first, a steady slide of them down her cheeks. He reached into his pocket and pulled out a velvet jeweler's box, took out a ring with hands that trembled and offered it up to her.

She knelt opposite him and spread the fingers of her left hand, watched him slide the beautiful ring onto her finger, mesmerized by the sparkle of diamonds and by the overwhelming significance of this moment.

Diamonds on her finger. From Seth, Mr. Fear of Commitment.

Diamonds. On her finger.

"Bonnie Fortuna, will you marry me?"

It took three tries for her voice to work. "Seth Blackstone, I would love to."

She kissed him, kissed him again, and even though she'd kissed this man dozens, hundreds, maybe thousands of times, these kisses felt brand-new, stronger and more intimate. Finally, after so much pain, so much growing, so much love, from that moment on, it would be the two of them, for each other, with each other, forever.

Oh, Seth.

13

"So AFTER THAT Dave was totally wasted. And this ugly chick comes on to him, but he's like, 'Sorry, I'm not into fat girls.' And she goes, 'You are drunk.' And he's like, 'Yeah, but in the morning I'll be sober and you'll still be fat.'" Nick burst into coarse laughter. "The guy is freaking brilliant."

Colin made a sound of disgust. "The guy is freaking plagiarizing Winston Churchill's joke."

He slowed his pace, monitoring his stride and posture. He and Nick were out running the Elliott Bay Trail again, and Colin was determined this time not to let his ego get in the way of his recovery. Knock wood, he'd had two pain-free weeks and was feeling stronger all the time.

Without the pain, sex with Demi was getting hotter and more adventurous and more emotional than anything he'd ever experienced. His whole life was different from anything he'd ever experienced.

"Churchill, huh. Well, it's still funny."

"Yeah, making people feel horrible about themselves is really hilarious."

"Dude, lighten up." Nick scowled at him. "And is that the fastest you can run, grandpa?"

"Yup." Everything about Nick was bugging him today.

He felt as if knowing Demi and meeting some of her friends had deepened and enriched his capacity for healthy relationships. What had he and Nick shared but training and bullshit boasting about women and partying? More to the point, why had that sustained Colin for so long?

It couldn't now.

"So, uh, thought you should know. Stephanie and I aren't together anymore."

Colin felt the very slightest twinge in his chest at that news. More like habit than anything else. "That was quick."

"She's seriously high maintenance. We're together two weeks and she starts acting like we're married."

"Yeah?" He was amused, he had to admit. Stephanie was seriously delusional if she was looking for commitment from Nick. "Like what?"

"Like expecting me to hold my weekends open for her, check with her every time I want to go out, like she holds the master schedule to my life. And man, she is even more competitive than I am. Like, 'You shouldn't be drinking that second beer, you have an event in less than a month.' I'm like, 'Chill out, I know my body.' You know? It's like my triathlon career is suddenly ours. Like it's more important than I am."

"Maybe it is." He tipped his face up to the sun, enjoying the faint warmth in the November chill. What if he'd given in and asked Stephanie to marry him? The accident had spared them both a lifetime of misery or divorce. *Silver linings, Demi.*

"She was talking a lot about you toward the end, though, man. I get the feeling she thinks she made a mistake."

"Yeah?" The news barely registered.

"So if you want her back, you better up your training." Nick threw Colin a contemptuous glance and pulled ahead. "At this pace your next Ironman won't be for three years."

"I'm not doing Ironmen anymore." He felt only a slight jab of regret. "I'll probably be able to do the sprint length, though."

"Sprints?" Nick scoffed. "A quarter-mile swim, twelve-mile bike, three-mile run? What kind of challenge is that?"

"Better than nothing." He found himself speeding up to stay abreast of Nick, and made himself slow. "I'll have more time to do other things."

"You can't be serious." Nick dropped back beside him, shaking his head. "You have lost it, dude."

Colin chuckled. Maybe someday Nick would wake up to a bigger world, but Colin doubted it. "Trust me, I found more than I lost."

"Come on. Are you serious? You live for this. We *all* do."

"I used to. There's other good stuff out there."

"What about Hawaii? What about being the best? You try hard, train hard, you can get back. What do the doctors know?"

For a second, Colin allowed the old visualization back, of himself ahead of the pack, approaching the finish line in Hawaii, fans cheering, women lusting, the championship in his grasp. His adrenaline raced, his gut tightened, his lips tensed in a determined curl, his stride quickened... and his back gave a warning throb.

He deliberately replaced the vision with one of himself wrapping Demi in his arms during a long-weekend getaway in the mountains or on the beach, her head on his shoulder, hair across his chest, her bright eyes gazing at him. His lips smoothed and curved in a smile. His gut relaxed. His back eased.

"Not doing that anymore. I have other goals now."

"Like what? Getting fat and sitting on your ass?"

"No, actually I'm going to ask Demi to marry me, buy a

house and have a boatload of kids and a dog. Get a graduate degree in business and start a new career as an executive."

Nick turned and ran sideways to gape at him. "Say *what?*"

Colin thought he'd have a hard time keeping the smile off his face, but that wasn't the case. At all. He'd deliberately picked the scenario Nick would least expect, but when the words started coming out of him, he was startled to find that they were true. His subconscious knew what he wanted more than he did. Marry Demi. Have kids. Share a house with her. Start a new career that used more brains than brawn. With her in his life, he felt as if anything was possible. "You heard me."

"What the hell would you want to do any of that for?"

Colin grinned, suddenly giddy with this entirely new vision. Coming home to Demi. Kissing their baby. Petting the dog. "What I want has changed."

"No kidding." Nick shook his head in despair. "Well, it's your funeral."

And there it was, the end of what turned out not to have been a beautiful friendship.

"I guess."

"I'll catch you coming back. I can't stand running this slow anymore." Nick took off at a pace Colin couldn't possibly match.

Yeah, Nick could leave him in the dust on any trail in the state, and probably would always be able to. But Colin was beginning to realize that he was the one truly pulling ahead.

"HI, COLIN." DEMI sat in her office, phone to her ear, grinning so hard it nearly hurt. Colin lit her up like a floodlight, a lightning bolt, Las Vegas—what else was bright enough? She could see him two hours after their last goodbye and feel as if it was a precious months-later reunion.

So she'd done it. Fallen in love. She thought she'd been in love before, but that had been nothing like this. Around Colin she felt strong, confident, not mousy, not worthless, not alien. Things that frightened her before she tossed off with a laugh. She and Carrie had even had a nice lunch together. They'd never be best friends, but there was a strong possibility of a real sister relationship evolving with her.

Having someone think you were the cat's meow, the bee's knees, a red-hot mama—well, it was hard to keep trying to convince yourself you were anything else. Because who wanted to?

And yet, there was so much to admire in Colin. It wasn't all about how he made her feel. She loved his courage, his determination. He was working regularly with Julie, making great progress, and he seemed to have accepted his new limitations much faster than she'd expected.

However.

There were no concrete signs on his part that he was falling in love with her, too.

Well, maybe there were some signs, but she didn't dare start looking or trying to interpret them, because the only thing worse than knowing your partner wasn't in love with you was spending agonizing time hoping he was.

"Meet me at Cal Anderson Park for lunch today? I want to buy you a hot dog. And I have a present for you."

"Oooh, a present! Yes, I would love to meet you, even without hot dogs *or* the expensive jewels."

"How did you know?"

She laughed. "And furs? And cruise tickets? I require all such things."

"I knew that about you." His voice was soft, tender, and sent shivers through her that were almost as deep and exciting as the sexual ones he induced in her. Quite regularly, in fact.

"What time?"

"I'm on my way. Be there in five, so as soon as you can make it…"

She glanced at her watch. "I'm finishing up some paperwork, so— Oh, guess what, I'm finished. I'll be right out."

His laughter felt like a prize she'd been awarded. They'd known each other six weeks, but she felt in many ways as if it had been much longer.

Stuffing the insurance forms back into their folder, Demi jumped up from her desk, locked her office and skipped down the hall, waving first at Bonnie, who actually waved back—she'd been acting as if she'd won the lottery lately, which she essentially had, thanks to Seth's video. And she had *almost* smiled at Demi the night before during another meeting on the holiday special gift cards, which would go on sale the next day in time for Thanksgiving.

On her right, a wave to Angela and then out the door into the cloudy chill of mid-November, which felt like a sunny day in Florida to her, because guess what? She was seeing Colin when she hadn't thought she would, and that was always a sunny-day kind of experience.

She nearly ran the last several feet toward the hot-dog cart where he was waiting, but made herself stay calm— *yes, yawn, hey, Colin, good to see you*—when she wanted to fling herself in his arms and kiss every inch of him, shrieking that she loved him and would for all time.

Good way to make a guy you're seeing casually feel totally comfortable.

However, when she was a foot away, he lunged at her and swung her around as if she weighed one hundred pounds, which she decidedly didn't. What an extra-nice perk, to have a boyfriend you weighed less around.

"Hi." He kissed her as if he hadn't seen her for a lifetime, when it had actually only been twenty-two hours, five minutes and thirty-two seconds. Or so.

"Hi." She was beaming like a fool, she knew it. Except that he was looking unusually animated, too, so that was fine.

And no, she was not going to read anything into it.

They ordered hot dogs from the same impassive man she'd ordered hot dogs from countless times, who never gave the slightest sign that he recognized her, no matter how friendly and chatty she tried to be.

The benches by the fountain were being used, so they perched on the pool's concrete edge, eating hot dogs and chatting comfortably about their days. Work was going well for Colin. He was back to a full schedule. Demi had gotten a new client with neck issues. They were thinking about going to see a movie that weekend.

She loved having someone to talk to every day. Boyfriends weren't everything in life, but they were really nice. Especially this one, who was close to her like no boyfriend she'd ever had. If only there were some magic place she could dial into and place an order for a guaranteed happy ending. Not that she was dying to get married—okay, the fantasy of marrying Colin had occurred to her and it had been exciting, even though she'd made sure to shut it down right away so she didn't start convincing herself that's what she wanted—but it would be nice not to have an end to this lovely association. Not to mention the lovely screaming-banshee sex. It added so much to life.

"Hey." He stuffed his trash into the paper sack the hot dogs came in and handed it over so she could add hers. "You ready for your present?"

"Well, of course." Her heart beat just a little faster, even as she sternly told herself it could be her favorite flavor of gum.

"Here." He drew a slim package out of his jacket, eyes full of something she couldn't quite identify.

It was probably not gum. "Thank you, Colin."

"You don't know what it is yet."

She started unwrapping, hands a bit shaky, emotions a bit shaky, telling herself over and over to stop imagining. "No, but I can thank you for the thought."

"You're welcome for the thought." His body was tense, which communicated to her that he really wanted her to like his gift, which made her tense, because she really wanted to like it, too, for his sake.

She lifted off the lid and gasped. A knife. No, a work of art. Long, slender shining blade without a single scratch, and a smooth red handle. She picked it up. The weight was perfect in her hand, expertly balanced and gracefully fitted to her grip.

"Colin, this is exquisite." She clutched it to her chest, near tears. "I can't believe how much work you must have put into this."

He was pleased. Really pleased. She could tell by the way his eyes softened, and his mouth tightened, as if he was trying to keep himself from looking anything but man-tough. "Glad you like it."

"No. I love it. Thank you. I'll use it a lot." She held it out admiringly. "Though I sort of feel as if I should put it under glass and display it."

"No. Use it. Enjoy it." He smiled in that way that made it seem the two of them were the only two people in the world, which at that moment, as far as she was concerned, they were.

"*Colin!* Wow! Hi!"

Demi started, then turned to see one of the most stunning blondes the universe had ever produced. Tall, slender, wearing a skintight running outfit that left no question to anyone with functioning vision that her figure was spectacular.

Demi hated her instantly.

"Stephanie." Colin stood up, smiling the held-back smile he'd just given Demi when he didn't want to show how pleased he was.

"It's *so* great to see you." She hesitated in this perfect oh-gosh sort of way and then stepped forward and kissed him, holding her lips on his cheek a little too long.

No, way too long.

Demi hated her more. And now that Colin was standing there, grinning and not introducing Demi, she sort of hated him, too.

"How are things going?" His voice had become low and gruff. With emotion?

"Fine. Fine." Stephanie brushed a piece of something off his chest that probably wasn't even there. "I broke up with Nick. Maybe you heard."

"He told me." He stuffed his hands into his pockets, which he did when he was uneasy.

Yup. Demi hated them both. And she felt dark and ugly and fat and in the way.

She wasn't supposed to feel that way around Colin.

"Stephanie, this is a friend of mine. Demi. She was my PT for a while."

Oh. Friend. PT. Not lover, not girlfriend. "Hi, Stephanie." Demi stood, feeling like the mutant next to Mr. and Mrs. Universe.

"Hi, Demi." Stephanie linked her arm through Colin's. "Thanks for helping get Colin here back on track."

"You're welcome." She picked up the box to put the knife away. Stephanie pounced.

"Oh, pretty one, Colin. Nick and I were comparing ours the other day. You gave one to Tom once, too, didn't you?"

Demi felt sick. Very nice, Stephanie. Really very nice. Make sure Demi was aware that there was less than no significance to the gift. Colin had probably given one to his garbage collector, too.

"I like making them." His voice was pleasant, but she could read the tension underneath, see it in his body as he extracted his arm from Stephanie's. He wanted one of them gone. Might as well be her. He and Stephanie must have lots of catching up to do. Especially because, guess what, she was available again, and made sure he knew it within the first ten seconds of their joyous meeting.

"I was actually wondering the other day if you'd like to get together sometime, Colin." Stephanie tossed her ponytail, blinked up at him enticingly in that way that only enticing women had. If Demi tried it she'd look as if she had something in her eye. "Talk things over?"

Demi closed her eyes, telling herself murder would only land her in jail and, anyway, she wasn't sure which of them she'd rather take out first.

"We do have plenty to talk about." At least Colin didn't sound warm and sexual the way Stephanie had.

"Why don't you talk now?" Demi put the knife away and rather pointedly handed the bag of trash to Colin. "I need to get back to the office."

"Okay." Colin gave her a perfunctory smile, hands cemented to his hips, barely meeting her eyes. "Thanks for lunch. Nice to see you again."

Nice to see her again? As if they'd just met up to discuss the good old days of his treatment? Ouch. Just ouch.

"Good to meet you, Stephanie. Thanks for the knife, Colin."

She nodded pleasantly to both of them and turned. Before she was out of earshot, she heard Stephanie asking if "that woman" was Colin's girlfriend. Immediately, she pretended her shoe needed adjusting so she'd be able to hear his answer.

It came quickly, in the form she half expected, though a stupid, eternally romantic part of her was hoping for something completely different.

"Demi? No, no, just a friend."

She fled the scene, knowing she had a long day and a long cry ahead of her.

But that was that. She knew where she stood. All dreams she had of getting serious with Colin were over. So either she could hang in there with him, knowing she'd never get what she wanted, growing increasingly unhappy, frustrated and bitter.

Or she could end it. Now. Because unless she'd misread what was going on back there, Colin was about to go back to the woman he belonged with.

COLIN STRODE DOWN Broadway, barely keeping himself from sprinting. He'd been angry before of course. Angry most of his childhood because his father clearly favored his intellectual and successful brothers. Angry when Stephanie dumped him. Angry when he had to give up his dream of running the Ironman in Hawaii. But nothing had felt like this. That Stephanie's body wasn't lying lifeless in the park—figuratively speaking—was only due to him wanting to avoid the mess and trauma. After he told her what he thought of her, which she richly deserved, he spent ten minutes or so listening to her trying to make dewy-eyed apologies and then, when those didn't work, screeching out what she thought of him.

Wow, he sure missed those manipulative hysterics. By golly who wouldn't?

Stephanie had gone out of her way to make Demi feel small, insignificant and less. Less attractive, less graceful, less important than she was. What a joke. Demi was ten times the woman Stephanie could ever hope to be. Not stopping her right then and there had been the hardest thing Colin had ever done. But he knew his ex well. Once she got a whiff of the fact that he and Demi were a couple, the claws she'd kept mostly sheathed would have sprung out to ten-foot lengths and slashed Demi to ribbons.

Seeing Demi's face fall when she didn't understand he was protecting her, when she must have thought he was pandering to Stephanie at her expense… Colin still wanted to rip something into unrecognizable pieces. Like Stephanie.

Deep breath. All was not lost. He'd make it up to Demi. He'd explain. He'd hope like hell that she'd understand, and if she didn't today, he'd spend however much time it took convincing her he was crazy about her. After that little display in the park she had every right to think he was fickle, two-faced and shallow. That he made knives by the dozens and tossed them around to anyone, when he'd put more time and love into her knife than anything he'd ever made. And just like that Stephanie had trivialized his gift.

She was good, he had to hand it to her.

Up to him now to prove to Demi that his feelings were much more than casual for her.

He passed Edwin's Jewelers, where she'd stood and talked about buying the necklace. He'd loved that—still did—about her, the whimsy, the unexpected twists, the way she gradually revealed the fun and the fire that burned underneath her cool exterior.

Yeah, he was serious about her. Very serious.

His furious stride slowed. He turned around, retraced his steps to the jewelry store. The necklace was still there, sparkling on the headless model.

He opened the door to the shop and strode inside. Demi

would want to know how serious. Right here in this shop, he had the perfect way to show her.

"HEY, DEMI, GUESS what?"

Demi turned wearily. Damn it, she was almost to safety, just outside the door of her apartment, in the act of unlocking it, and look who showed up. About the last person she wanted to see besides Stephanie or Colin. Bonnie, looking as perky as Stephanie, only shorter and wearing a brightly flowered shirtdress. "What?"

"I wasn't sure you knew." She held up her left hand, fingers wiggling. "I thought I told you, but Angela said you didn't know yet. Seth and I are engaged!"

Demi tried to summon every bit of enthusiasm she could even though she was about to burst into tears. "That's great, Bonnie. Congratulations."

She frowned. "You don't seem that happy."

"No, I am. I'm just not in the greatest mood."

"Uh… Yeah, that's what I meant." She looked at Demi as if she only had half a brain. "Which is why I said, 'You don't seem that happy.'"

"Sorry." She put her hands to her temples, sure her head was about to crack into pieces. "I thought you meant I hadn't seemed excited enough."

"Yikes." Bonnie actually looked horrified. "That would have been horrible."

Nothing new from you. "When are you getting married?"

"*Soon.* Like next month." She tried to scowl but there was no way her joy could be covered up completely. "Before the jerk changes his mind."

"He won't."

"And you know about Jack and Melissa's engagement?"

"Jack told me, yes." She struggled to put on a look of delight. "That's great, too."

"You're the only one left!" Bonnie folded her arms over her chest, beaming. "We gotta do something about that."

"*No.* God no." Demi couldn't hold her tears back another second, and when they came, they came in torrents. *Crap.* She turned and blindly tried to locate her doorknob. "I'm sorry."

"Demi, oh, my God." Bonnie followed her inside, the last thing Demi wanted her to do. "There I was completely ignoring the fact that you're miserable, and telling you all this good news, when you'd *told* me you were miserable. But did I take the hint? No. *I'm* the one who's sorry."

"It's okay. But…" Demi gestured back toward the door. "I think I need to be alone now."

"No." Bonnie shook her head. "That is absolutely the last thing you need. I will make you some tea and you will tell me everything. And if you don't want me, I'll get Angela, because she will… Oh, wait. She's working."

Demi sighed, feeling trapped. "Is Bonnie Blooms closed?"

"I hired an assistant," Bonnie announced proudly. "Or more like an apprentice. This wonderful older lady who needs to get out of the house. She works for pretty much nothing."

"That's nice." Her voice broke. More tears.

Bonnie clapped her hand to her mouth, green eyes contrite. "Gah, here I go again blabbering on about me. Now. We're going to fix you. Where is your tea?"

Demi numbly pointed to the cabinet. She didn't have the energy to get into it with Bonnie, and frankly, if Bonnie was finally going to be nice, she didn't want to discourage her. When Colin dumped her she'd need all the friends she could get.

"I assume this has to do with Colin."

"Of course."

"Of course." Bonnie filled the kettle, rolling her eyes.

"How much do we suffer over these damn guys? I wish I knew why we find them irresistible. Life would be so much simpler without them."

"True." Demi stared glumly down at her table, chin propped on her hands, wondering if it was possible to die of a broken heart anywhere outside of an opera.

"Now, what has Colin done that would give the Come to Your Senses crowd license to remove his privates?"

More tears, along with the ghost of a giggle at Bonnie's humor. "His old girlfriend showed up."

"Ooh." Bonnie's face crumpled with sympathy. "Those encounters are the worst. Seth had so many old girlfriends, it happened every time we stepped out of the building."

"I think they're going to get back together."

"Think?" Bonnie jammed her hands onto her hips. "So you're not sure yet?"

Demi told her the story of what had happened in the park, feeling stronger as Bonnie's outrage grew. "That bastard."

"I just can't believe I judged him so wrong." She took the tissue Bonnie handed her and wiped her eyes. "I'm usually good at weeding out the real jerks."

"Yeah?" Bonnie contemplated her thoughtfully. "Well, I can't see how you could have misunderstood the situation, but if your instinct told you this guy was a good one… maybe you should hold off on total despair until you hear his version of the story."

"Maybe."

Bonnie wrinkled her nose. "I admit it doesn't sound good. But even if the worst happens, you still have us."

"Yeah." Demi rolled her eyes. "And you're all engaged."

"Ew, I forgot. That is brutal." She patted Demi's hand, then jumped up. "Mugs?"

"There." She pointed to the cabinet by the sink. My God,

the woman had enough energy to power a windmill. She was exhausting. And also serving as Demi's lifeline to sanity at the moment, for which she was grateful.

"So, by the way, I was pretty awful to you for a long time, Demi. I'm sorry." Bonnie got down two mugs. "I thought you were stuffy and standoffish. You never hung out with us. I thought you had decided we were beneath you."

"I'm just shy."

"That's what Angela said. I have to tell you, she and Jack really whupped me upside the head. Said they'd been spending more time with you and that I was wrong about you and better try to make more of an effort."

"You're doing a bang-up job." The remark came out drily. She couldn't help it.

To her amazement, Bonnie cracked up and turned, still grinning. "Okay, I'm not the most subtle person in the world."

Demi managed a smile, which to her surprise was genuine. "Maybe not. But it's sweet of you to want to help me."

The kettle started screaming. Bonnie grabbed it and filled their mugs, set them on the table.

"I just want you to know if this Colin guy turns out to be the world's biggest jerk, you've got friends here who have your back and always will. I'm going to include myself in that category, too." She picked up her mug and held it up. "Here's to looking forward."

"To looking forward," Demi said. "Which suits me because I don't ever want to think about what happened back in the park again."

Bonnie's gaze jerked suddenly over Demi's head. At the same time, Demi registered the sound of her front door opening. Hadn't she locked it? She always locked it.

"Uh-oh." Bonnie looked like she'd seen a ghost. And

right then Demi knew exactly who was standing behind her, and that her hopes of never having to think about what happened in the park again were about to be crushed under a well-worn size-twelve running shoe.

14

DEMI STOOD INVOLUNTARILY. If Bonnie hadn't grabbed the tea out of her hand, she would have let the mug fall. Colin was here. Her heart rose in her chest until it felt as if it was trying to burst into her throat.

Not a pleasant feeling.

Worse, her brain was registering that he looked about six times as gorgeous as he had any right to, his dark eyes deep and somber, his jaw set, hair windblown. Poor Colin was going to have quite the time dumping her. How he must dread it.

What would he say?

Stephanie and I have so much in common and...

When I saw her today it hit me like a thunderbolt that we're meant to be together...

You and I have always known this was temporary...

It's not you, it's me...

Okay, if he said that last one she was going to kick him where it counted.

"Hi." He stood in her entranceway, hands in his pockets. When his eyes met hers, his face registered shock, then froze into grim stone.

She looked that good, huh.

"I'm Bonnie." Bonnie strode over to him, huge smile in place, and shook his hand.

"I'm Col—"

"I know who you are." She beamed harder, her voice superperky. "And I just want you to know that the four of us living here with Demi take the whole friendship thing very seriously, so if you hurt her, we're going to hunt you down with machetes. Okay?"

Colin glanced past Bonnie at Demi, who found herself out of the kitchen without having been aware she'd moved. Colin was probably wondering what the hell she'd told Bonnie—he didn't know she'd overheard his dismissive comment about her. Demi couldn't feel bad about it. She couldn't feel much of anything. She wanted this over with, wanted him out of here, wanted Bonnie out of here and wanted to collapse into pain for a few months and then get over it. Maybe she'd close her practice for a month and fly to Jamaica to grieve on the beach.

"Machetes. Well. I'm glad Demi has friends who care about her so much." Colin smiled down at Bonnie with distinct affection. Bonnie sent Demi a what-the-heck? look that Demi would have responded to if she'd been able to move.

"Okay, then." Bonnie took a couple of steps back, arms still folded, eyes narrowed in suspicion. "I'll give you two some privacy, but I'm *right* down the hall."

She strode to the door, turning behind Colin to give Demi a look of melting sympathy and a thumbs-up for courage. Then she left. The door closed behind her.

"Would you like to sit in the living room?" Demi gestured him in, feeling like a zombie hostess.

"Demi." He took two steps toward her, reached toward her cheek. She ducked away and headed for the couch.

"We can talk in here."

"You've been crying." His voice was anguished. "That sucked in the park today. The way Stephanie treated you, the way I treated you. I'm sorry it had to be like that."

"I understand." Rock. She was made of rock. Except rock wouldn't know that emotional agony was on its way soon. Rock was very lucky in that it didn't have to feel anything at all. She'd like to stay made of rock for as long as possible. Like maybe until she'd gotten over Colin and was happy again.

"No, you don't understand." He made as if to sit next to her on the couch.

"There." She pointed across the room to a chair, teal with gold, which Carrie had bought in her striped-furniture phase, then decided she didn't like the shape. "You sit over there."

He pressed his lips together, then went to his assigned seat. "Okay."

"Good." No, she wasn't made of rock. Metal. Metal parts. She was a robot.

She wished.

Colin leaned toward her, hands folded, elbows on his thighs. Oh, those thighs. She didn't want them to belong to that woman. "Here's the thing about Stephanie."

Demi's face actually twitched when he said Stephanie. She knew what "the thing" was about Stephanie. She was perfect. "Okay."

"I know her really well."

Yes, and you also know she's perfect for you, so you'll have a perfect wedding and raise perfect brats who will torment you their entire lives.

A girl could always hope. "Okay."

"Stephanie has always been and will always be—"

"Perfect."

"No." Colin looked startled. "Stephanie has always been and will always be about Stephanie."

Demi blinked. That's why he still loved her? That was weird. She wouldn't have thought Colin would fall for someone who—

Her brain screeched as it tried furiously to work again. Wait…

"And I knew if she found out we're a couple…" He shook his head. "Well, let's put it this way. You saw how snarky she was. If I'd let on how I feel about you, she would have turned it up a thousand percent. She can be truly vicious."

We're a couple… How I feel about you…

Demi blinked again and managed to move her head. Deep in her chest, she felt little stirrings of hope. "After I started walking away, you told her I was nothing to you."

"Oh, Demi." He winced as if she'd socked him. "I'm so sorry you heard that. I was protecting me by that time. You have not seen tantrums until you've seen Stephanie's. I wanted to make sure you were far gone before she started."

He was acting so normal. As if nothing had changed between them. "So…you aren't going back to her?"

"God no." Colin shuddered. "Not in a million years."

"Does she know that?"

"Oh, yes. As soon as you were safely away, she found out. I have the hearing damage to prove it." He got to his feet, smile fading. "I hated putting you through that, Demi. I'm sorry she tried to cheapen the knife. The truth is, I only make knives for people and friends I love. And I'm grateful the hilt isn't sticking out of my back right now. I wouldn't blame you."

"I thought about it." Her features allowed the beginnings of a grin. They were just friends. She shouldn't take the *L*-word too literally. "So is this woman going to come after me?"

"No." He sat next to Demi on her couch. Without her permission. Took her hand. Also without her permission.

"She calms down after she's vented. Also, um, I might have said something vaguely threatening."

His hand was warm and dry and comforting; her body and brain started a slow, delicious thaw. "Vaguely threatening?"

"Yeah, you know, implying that it would not be a good idea to bother you."

"I see." She smiled for real; he squeezed her hand. "How did you imply that?"

"Something along the lines of, 'If you go near Demi I'll have Bonnie hunt you down with machetes.'"

She actually laughed that time, and boy did it feel good to have her humanity returning. Except she still wasn't clear on what was going to happen between them, or how they'd go forward. She loved him. His feelings were a big question mark. "So what now, Colin?"

"Now?" He looked very serious. "Now I want to make love to you until you come so loudly all the people in your building call 9-1-1."

"Oh." She got up off the couch, away from temptation. "I'm not sure that's such a—"

"Demi." He stood, too, and pulled her into his arms. "Where is your can-do attitude?"

"I'm not sure." To her horror, tears formed. Again. She still had Colin, which was really good, but maybe only for sex, which was bad. She'd almost lost Colin to Stephanie, which was terrible, and then she didn't, which was good. She loved Colin, which was good, but wasn't sure she could keep him, which was bad.

It had been a long, confusing day. And it wasn't even dinnertime yet.

"Sweetheart." He tucked her head against his shoulder and held her with his strong arms, rocking her back and forth. "I'm so sorry."

For a while she burrowed against him, eyes closed, relishing his strength and familiar smell. Then practical Demi took over. Did she want to get this close again, get used to relying on him, risk falling more deeply in love with him, when the payoff could be getting her heart smashed anyway?

But his mouth found hers, and she surrendered to the sheer bliss of the contact. And then he murmured such sweet and tender things that her stupid hope burned brighter. Maybe he'd grow to love her, too, over the next weeks and months. If she bolted now, she'd never give them that chance.

She deepened their kiss, began exploring the sleek contours of his back and shoulders with her hands, with her mouth, her favorite place between the firm curves of his pecs, pressing her pelvis against him, wanting to lose herself in this man's body and his desire for her.

Their passion mounted, kisses turned fiery, and fingers fumbled with clothing until they were naked, hands all over each other, and Demi finally got so hot she turned in his arms, braced herself against the wall and offered herself to him, needing the rush, the crazy burn of animal ecstasy.

His hands followed the upward line of her arms to rest over her fingers. His body was warm against her back, his penis slid between her legs without entering her. He took her hands from the wall, turned her to look at him. "Not this way. Not today."

She stared back, unsure what he meant.

"Come." He led her into her bedroom. At the edge of the bed he drew her close again, kissed her forehead, her cheeks, her mouth, over and over, slow, gentle, sweet kisses.

Demi felt cherished, adored...but while half of her was saying yes, yes, that this was what she wanted, the other half was retreating, fearful of the vulnerability this exquisite tenderness engendered.

He helped her onto the bed, where there were more kisses, and a long, leisurely exploration of her body with his fingers and his mouth. Gradually she relaxed into this slow, languid pace and allowed herself to open, mindful of the risk, but as always loving the honesty and depth of their connection.

He slid on top of her, kissing her, murmuring endearments she wouldn't ever have imagined could come out of the mouth of her cranky triathlete six weeks ago. She wrapped her arms around his neck, his back, his shoulders, making sure he knew how much she loved the feel of him against her, the warm sweep of his skin, his smell and his taste. For a long, long time they lay like that, just touching, exploring, sharing themselves physically and emotionally to a degree that eclipsed even their previous lovemaking.

Then he put on a condom and lay back over her, one hand pressed to her cheek, eyes steadily on hers, and pushed deep inside her. Demi disappeared into his eyes, into the dreamy intensity of their lovemaking, sure she'd never shared this kind of intimacy with anyone ever before.

Colin.

She had no idea how long they were there, lazily making love, hands never still, arousal constant but in the background as she luxuriated in how tied she felt to this man.

Then finally the background became the foreground, their movements faster. Desperation crept in, up to the final sweep of ecstasy. Colin held back until she went over the edge, then let himself go with her, holding the pleasure between them as long as they possibly could.

With him, Demi understood what sex could be about. Her previous experiences had been shallow imitations of what could happen between two people. She was so grateful to Colin for showing her how much better it could be.

He lifted his head to meet her eyes, and the awe in them was such that she realized Colin hadn't showed her anything. This was something they'd discovered together. This belonged only to them.

Her heart lifted.

"Demi," he whispered.

"Yes."

"That was…" He shook his head, bewildered. "I don't know where we went, but I've never been there before."

"Me neither." She let everything she felt show in her eyes. And there was a hell of a lot.

He moved restlessly. "I have something to give you."

"No." She wasn't ready to let him move yet. "You just gave me the knife a few hours ago. And the best sex of my life a few minutes ago. I don't need anything else."

"Stephanie tainted the knife."

"No." She shook her head. "Absolutely not. I'm always going to treasure it."

He moved off her, sent her a mischievous look. "Well, I'm not taking this present back, so you're stuck."

"Oh, for—" Demi rolled her eyes. "You are so selfish."

"Aren't I?" He drew his hand down her cheek, kissed her lingeringly, then strode out of the room, his body beautiful enough to inspire a sculptor.

He was hers. For only a while, maybe. But hers now.

He came back in, holding a long, thin box, eyebrows up with worry, body tense, exactly as he'd been in the park.

"Another knife?"

"I didn't make this."

"Colin, you're really going to make me feel like I…" Her voice trailed off. She'd seen the box up close. Edwin's Jewelers.

He saw her staring. "Remember when we looked in the window together?"

She gaped at him. He hadn't. Not the necklace. It cost thousands. He couldn't possibly have.

"Remember that necklace you showed me?"

"Colin." She could barely breathe, let alone speak. "You did not buy me that necklace."

"Nope." He grinned and knelt by the bed, placed the box in front of her. "I bought you something else."

"You…" She smacked him playfully. "Don't ever do that again."

"What, buy you jewelry?"

"No, pretend you did." She reached for the lid. "If you'd bought me something that expensive I would have had to—"

She stopped. This time she really couldn't speak. Or breathe. In the box, cleverly attached to keep it from sliding around, was a ring.

No, she was seeing things. It was…

A ring. A diamond ring. The kind a man bought for a woman when he was—

She lifted her eyes to his face, not daring to interpret even this completely obvious…

Ring.

"Demi." His voice came out husky and low. "I've never met anyone who has brought as much to my life as you have. I've never met anyone who inspires me so much, who makes me so happy and so…hot all the time."

A giggle-sob escaped her.

"I admire your talent, your humor, your outlook, your in-cred-ible body, and I can't ever envision a time when I won't want to turn to you, talk to you, make love to you. I love you. Will you marry me?"

She nodded. And then she nodded again. And she really,

really tried to think of something to say that would even come close to the beautiful speech he'd just given, that would encapsulate her feelings so perfectly, show him how important he was to her, how much she admired and adored him.

But all that came out of her was happy tears and one word: "Yes."

His face crumped into relief, he climbed onto the bed and they wrapped themselves around each other as if they'd never, ever let go.

And Demi stopped worrying about telling him all the things she wanted him to know, outlining perfectly all the remarkable and beautiful things he'd done for her and brought to her.

Because she realized she'd have the rest of her natural life to get it absolutely right.

Epilogue

Postmark: Rockport, Maine

Dear Extended Come to Your Senses Family,
Seth and I are loving our honeymoon here in Maine.
The only problem is figuring out how many lobsters
we should eat at every meal. No, really, including
breakfast. This is one of the most gorgeous places
on earth, but we still miss you all and can't wait to
come home. Okay, Seth says that's ridiculous. We
can definitely wait to get home, but it will be easier
to leave this place knowing the rest of you will be
coming back from your adventures, too. Best idea
ever to close Come to Your Senses for quadruple
honeymoons. As long as our customers and clients
don't forget us! Oh, one more thing, Seth was hired
to score that big Hollywood movie even though we
can't tell you who the actor is playing the lead, but if
it works out, I'm going to want to cheat on Seth big-

time. He is making me tell you I'm kidding. Like you couldn't tell.

Love to you all from paradise,
Bonnie

Postmark: Paris

Bonjour, mes amis,
Well, Daniel and I are not going to make it back from Paris, I am sorry to tell you, because we have eaten so much croissant and pastry that the plane will charge us for our overweight butts and we can't afford it. Everything is so ooh-la-la around us, elegant and beautiful, ancient and new, fascinating and delicious. And boy, it's ten times better being here this time with a husband who adores me. Definitely do not recommend marrying ones who don't. Tonight we're going to splurge on dinner at one of the best restaurants in town, which will set us back the price of a small Latin American country, but hey, you only live once. Somehow, even in this fabulous romantic city with this fabulous romantic man, I still manage to miss you guys.

À bientôt, mes bien-aimés,
Angela

Postmark: Athens

Hey all, having a wonderful time. Glad you're not here. I thought I'd seen Melissa at her most beautiful at the wedding, but photographing her against the backdrop of this incredible place, with the clear water and stunning monuments, makes me realize how wrong I was. You think you know someone well enough to marry her, and then after the ceremony you realize a whole new depth of intimacy is now possible, and that fifty or sixty years might not be enough time to explore it all. And in case that was too sentimental we had our first fight—over who got to pose with the juggling monkey. Brutal! I won of course. Oops. She just told me to stop being a lying pig. She won. I caved. I've never been happier, and it's great thinking that the same has to be true for all of you. We'll have great stories to tell in September and for the rest of our lives.

Be at peace,
Jack.

Postmark: Kailua-Kona, Hawaii

Dear Angela, Daniel, Bonnie, Seth, Jack and Melissa,

I love this idea of coming home to letters from each other. But I can't say I love the idea of coming home. Not right this minute because I'm writing this on the beach next to the hottest man on the island. No, really. He's sweating like a pig.

So my control-freak husband wouldn't tell me where we were going on our honeymoon until we got to the airport. Such a typical guy. Didn't occur to him I would need to know climate information to pack. Prepare for anything, he says. Big help.

Hawaii is stunning. We're here now visiting the site of the Ironman World Championships. I'm proud to say Colin only broke down sobbing twelve or thirteen times. Okay, no, wait. He says make sure I tell you that manly men like him don't cry. Ever.

Unless I withhold sex.

Being away from you all has made me appreciate

our partnership and friendship all the more, even though I was kind of a late bloomer in that regard. Yeah, okay, wallflower nerd. But I look forward to the years to come, to more holiday events like the last one, which went so well, to more successes, joys and, hey, who's going to have the first baby?

Thanks to all of you, and here's to the bright happy future we're all going to share.

See you soon!

xoxox

Demi

* * * * *

COMING NEXT MONTH from Harlequin® Blaze™
AVAILABLE OCTOBER 16, 2012

#717 THE PROFESSIONAL
Men Out of Uniform
Rhonda Nelson

Jeb Anderson might look like an angel, but he's a smooth-tongued devil with a body built for sin. Lucky for massage therapist Sophie O'Brien, she knows just what to do with a body like that....

#718 DISTINGUISHED SERVICE
Uniformly Hot!
Tori Carrington

It's impossible to live in a military town without knowing there are few things sexier than a man in uniform. Geneva Davis believes herself immune...until hotter than hot Marine Mace Harrison proves that a military man *out* of uniform is downright irresistible.

#719 THE MIGHTY QUINNS: RONAN
The Mighty Quinns
Kate Hoffmann

When Ronan Quinn arrives in Sibleyville, Maine, he finds not just a job, but an old curse, a determined matchmaker and a beautiful woman named Charlie. But is earth-shattering sex enough to convince him to give up the life he's built in Seattle?

#720 YOURS FOR THE NIGHT
The Berringers
Samantha Hunter

P.I. in training Tiffany Walker falls head-over-heels in lust for her mentor, sexy Garrett Berringer. But has she really found the perfect job *and* the perfect man?

#721 A KISS IN THE DARK
The Wrong Bed
Karen Foley

Undercover agent Cole MacKinnon hasn't time for a hookup until he rescues delectable Lacey Delaney after her car breaks down. But how can he risk his mission—even to keep the best sex of his life?

#722 WINNING MOVES
Stepping Up
Lisa Renee Jones

Jason Alright and Kat Moore were young and in love once, but their careers tore them apart. Now, fate has thrown them together again and given them one last chance at forever. But can they take it?

You can find more information on upcoming Harlequin® titles, free excerpts and more at www.Harlequin.com.

HBCNM1012

REQUEST YOUR FREE BOOKS!
2 FREE NOVELS PLUS 2 FREE GIFTS!

◆ Harlequin® *Blaze*™

red-hot reads!

HB11B

*Bestselling Harlequin® Blaze™ author Rhonda Nelson
is back with yet another irresistible Man out of Uniform.
Meet Jebb Willington—former ranger, current security
agent and all-around good guy. His assignment—to catch
a thief at an upscale retirement residence. The problem—
he's falling for sexy massage therapist Sophie O'Brien,
the woman he's trying to put behind bars....*

*Read on for a sneak peek at
THE PROFESSIONAL*

Available November 2012 only from Harlequin Blaze.

Oh, hell.

Former ranger Jeb Willingham didn't need extensive
army training to recognize the telltale sound that emerged
roughly ten feet behind him. He was Southern, after all,
and any born-and-bred Georgia boy worth his salt would
recognize the distinct metallic click of a 12-gauge shotgun.
And given the decided assuredness of the action, he knew
whoever had him in their sights was familiar with the gun
and, more important, knew how to use it.

"On your feet, hands where I can see them," she ordered.
He had to hand it to her. Sophie O'Brien was cool as a cu-
cumber. Her voice was steady, not betraying the slightest bit
of fear. Which, irrationally, irritated him. He was a strange
man trespassing on her property—she ought to be afraid,
dammit. Why hadn't she stayed in the house and called 911
like a normal woman?

Oh, right, he thought sarcastically. Because she wasn't
a *normal* woman. She was kind and confident, fiendishly
clever and sexy as hell.

He wanted her.

And the hell of it? Aside from the conflict of interest and the tiny matter of *her name at the top of his suspect list?*

She didn't like him.

"Move," she said again, her voice firmer. "I'd rather not shoot you, but I will if you don't stand up and turn around."

Beautiful, Jeb thought, feeling extraordinarily stupid. He'd been an army ranger, one of the fiercest soldiers among Uncle Sam's finest…and he'd been bested by a massage therapist with an Annie Oakley complex.

With a sigh, he got up and flashed a grin at her. "Evening, Sophie. Your shrubs need mulching."

She gasped, betraying the first bit of surprise. It was ridiculous how much that pleased him. "You?" she breathed. "What the hell are you doing out here?"

He pasted a reassuring look on his face and gestured to the gun still aimed at his chest. "Would you mind lowering your weapon? It's a bit unnerving."

She brought the barrel down until it was aimed directly at his groin. "There," she said, a smirk in her voice. "Feel better?"

Has Jebb finally met his match? Find out in
THE PROFESSIONAL

Available November 2012
wherever Harlequin Blaze books are sold.